BEWITCH YOU A MERRY CHRISTMAS

BRIMSTONE BAY MYSTERIES - BOOK 3

N.M. HOWELL

DUNGEON MEDIA CORP.

This is a **work of fiction**. Names, characters, businesses, places, events, and incidents are either the products of the author's imagination or used in a fictitious manner. Any resemblance to actual persons, living or dead, or actual events is purely coincidental.

No part of this publication may be reproduced, stored in a retrieval system, or transmitted, in any form or in any means – by electronic, mechanical, photocopying, recording or otherwise – without prior written permission.

Copyright © 2016 Dungeon Media Corp.

All rights reserved.

CHAPTER ONE

Launching myself onto the ground, I barrel-rolled to the side, barely avoiding the imminent attack.

A moment later, the air rushed above me. Another shot narrowly missed my head. Dodging sideways, I ran to hide behind a nearby tree. I could hear impact as the tree was hit. I swore under my breath.

Exhaling deeply to try and quiet my breath, I listened for movement around me. Unfortunately, the thick snow muffled the sound of footsteps.

It was late afternoon, and the sun cast long shadows on the snowy ground. I squinted into the bright light trying to make out where my attackers were.

The air was quiet, and I saw no sign of movement, so I peeked carefully around the tree.

I quickly retreated as I detected motion nearby, pressing my back firmly up against the thick trunk of the tree.

Another loud thud sounded as the tree was hit again.

"She's over here," a voice yelled. "We've got her surrounded."

They were coming for me. There was no way to escape.

"Back off," I yelled. "No fair. It's three against one!"

I covered my head as another massive snowball made its way towards me.

"That's what you get for eating the last of Mrs. Pots' sugar cookies," Bailey shouted at me from across the yard.

"I was saving you from the calories," I yelled back. "Don't want you to get fat!"

I laughed to myself but was then hit sideways across the head by a snowball that came right out of left field.

"Look who's talking," Rory yelled from behind a tree to my left.

"Cookie stealer," Jane shouted. I looked behind me and saw her running crouched behind the fence, doing her best to avoid my snowball attack.

I narrowed my eyes and covered my head, trying to figure out who had thrown the snowball that had made impact.

"You're all going down!" Three against one was hardly fair.

"Thief," Bailey yelled.

"Cookie hog," I yelled back.

It was a running joke between myself and my three housemates about Bailey and the local baker's cookies. Our landlady, Mrs. Brody, often chastised Bailey about her eating habits and her obsession with Mrs. Pots' baking. Mrs. Pots owned the local bakery in Brimstone Bay and made the world's best cookies.

Bailey was tall and thin, and extremely healthy and fit. But, man, did she like to eat. That girl could eat ten dozen cookies in one sitting and never gain a pound. It drove the rest of us crazy! Well, it drove me crazy, at least. I eat one cookie, and I swear I put on five pounds instantly.

After the many times Mrs. Brody told Bailey to stop eating, it had become a bit of a joke between us.

I grabbed a handful of snow and ran behind a nearby bush. Doing my best to be stealthy, I packed the snow into a giant ball and eyed my surroundings, looking for my next target.

Rory and Jane were behind the trees, but I could see the top of Bailey's blond head poking up behind a pile of snow about fifteen feet in front of me.

I whispered an incantation into my snowball, and the sweet smell of sugar cookies began emanating from its surface.

"Still want that cookie?" I shouted from behind the bush.

My opponents remained silent, but I could still see the top of Bailey's head.

Quietly, I moved towards the pile of snow, crouching down low so she didn't see my approach.

I then ran sideways when I got close enough, and threw the cookie-scented snowball at Bailey, striking her right in the face.

"HEY!" she shouted at me, kicking a pile of snow in my direction. "That's cheating."

"How is that cheating?" I called behind me as I ran back to the bush for safety. "You should pay better attention."

"Oh, is that sugar cookie?" she asked. I saw Bailey take a bite of the snow, then spit it out. "Ow, my teeth. Cold!"

"No kidding," I laughed.

"Uh-oh," I heard Rory yell. Her head appeared from behind the large tree she had been using for cover.

"I think we have company," Jane finished.

I looked towards the house where their gazes were directed towards and saw Mrs. Brody walk out into the snow in her housecoat.

She was a sight to see, that was for sure. She had recently changed her hair from a light pink to an electric blue, and it stood out on end like she had been shocked by lightning. She was a tiny woman, standing barely over four-feet tall, but what she lacked in height she certainly made up for in attitude.

The way she was marching out towards us, I knew something was coming.

"RUN!" Rory shouted.

"What?" I turned to look at her and saw about a hundred massive snowballs rise from the ground around us.

"Oh no," Bailey said. "RUN!"

We all turned to run away from the house, but I knew we were too late.

Hundreds of massive snowballs began flying towards us, chasing us farther away from the house towards the bluff.

"Who ate the last cookie?" Mrs. Brody called to us from behind the flying wall of snowballs.

Bailey turned to look at me as we ran, and my eyes widened in fear.

"Oh, damn," I said. "NOT ME!"

I ran faster, not wanting to face the wrath of a hungry, cookie-deprived Mrs. Brody.

We didn't stand a chance against her magic, though, and soon the snowballs caught up to us.

"DIVE!" Jane yelled.

I dove down into the snow and covered my eyes.

Snowballs began pummeling down on me, and before I knew it, I was blanketed in a massive pile of cold, wet snow.

"Not fair," I called to Mrs. Brody through the snow.

"That should teach you for stealing the last cookie," she snapped back at me.

I pushed the snow off of me and rolled over onto my back. The sky was clear, and it was one of those rare sunny winter days. I stretched my arms and legs out into the snow and made a snow angel as I regained my breath from my failed escape.

I closed my eyes and relished in the warm sun as it thawed my snow-frozen skin.

I had spent the past few years living in New York City, and while there was lots of snow there in the winter, it never really stuck. The streets were slushy, and the snow quickly turned an unappealing shade of gray.

I would sometimes make the trek into Central Park to enjoy the finer moments of winter, but with my busy school schedule at NYU, those days were few and far between.

This morning, the yard was covered in a beautiful thick layer of glistening snow. The perfectly smooth surface was short lived when my housemates attacked me with unfair advantage after I ate the last cookie from Mrs. Pots' latest delivery.

The air was quiet, and I could hear the light crashing of waves from the bay behind me, down below the bluffs at the back of the yard.

I sighed and breathed in the sweet scent of the

crisp winter air, enjoying a much needed moment of quiet.

The peace was short-lived, though, as a loud meowing sounded from behind me.

I tilted my head back to see an extremely fat Momma Cat waddling towards me, followed by her kitten Agnes.

Both cats had joined our little family two months ago in October, when I found them lurking within the walls of the old Victorian home we all shared. Between those two and Soot, my other little gray adopted furbaby, the house was getting quite full.

"Have you been dipping into the cookies, too?" I asked the fat white cat as she walked past me.

The poor cat was getting fatter by the day, and she waddled as she made her way through the snow. "You're lucky you escaped the wrath of Mrs. Brody."

Momma Cat meowed in response, then continued on her way. She obviously had better things to do than listen to me blabber on outside in the cold.

Or so I thought. She stopped and sat down in the snow just past my feet and began meowing loudly at me.

I sat up and looked at her. "What's going on, Momma?"

The cat meowed.

"Something wrong with Momma?" Bailey asked

as she walked over to me, brushing the snow out of her hair.

Mrs. Brody had given up her attack and gone back into the house.

I shrugged. "I'm not sure. She seems fine. Just a bit fat. Maybe we should lay off the food."

"Aw but she's so cute and pudgy," Bailey said.

I laughed and nodded. "Fat little ball of fur. Looks just like you."

Bailey kicked more snow at me, and I wiped it away from my face as I laughed.

"Better get inside before our hands freeze off," I said.

I took Bailey's hand, and we walked into the house, followed by Jane and Rory.

Mrs. Pots had asked us to come help out at the bakery that night. It was the day before Christmas Eve, and she needed help re-organizing the Christmas displays, which usually just meant she needed help finishing up her Christmas cookie stock, apparently. Either way, I was looking forward to it.

Since moving to Brimstone Bay, my life had taken an odd turn. I'd been involved in solving a number of murders that occurred locally, and I was grateful the past month and a half were relatively quiet and normal.

Work has been busy, mostly because my editor was away on stress leave. Her romantic partner, and former Brimstone Press employee, was unfortunately killed this past Halloween.

I was happy to help out and was grateful for the promotion to lead journalist, but running the weekly paper was more work than I anticipated.

Fortunately, I arranged for this week's paper to be completed over a week ago, so everyone at the office could enjoy a week's vacation over Christmas.

I was looking forward to being lazy and doing absolutely nothing for Christmas, apart from drinking eggnog, eating cookies, and reading a good book. Oh, and hanging out with my new boyfriend Jordan, of course.

It took us a while given the odd circumstances of the beginning of our relationship, mostly due to the murders that kept occurring in town after we met, but he finally officially asked me out last month, and I was enjoying calling him my boyfriend. It made the idea of spending Christmas here in Brimstone Bay just a little bit less lonely.

"You ready?" Bailey called downstairs to me a few hours later.

I sat on my bed staring down at the fat ball of fur that lay sprawled on my floor, meowing up at me.

"I think I might sit tonight out," I called back.

Momma Cat meowed again.

The floors creaked as Bailey came bounding down the stairs. "What do you mean? It's your first

Christmas here, you have to come gorge with us at Mrs. Pots' so you can join in on the tradition!"

"I think there's something wrong with Momma," I said.

Bailey stared down at the cat, who rolled onto her other side and continued with her incessant meowing.

I sighed. "I don't think I should leave her alone."

"Look at you, being all maternal and stuff," Bailey Laughed.

I shrugged. "I've grown fond of these little brats. Who knew I'd become one of those crazy old cat ladies so soon."

"Alright, stay with her for now. But you really should come later. We'll be cracking the eggnog at midnight, so you better be there."

"Midnight?" I gaped. "What are you guys even doing over there?"

Bailey laughed. "Well, the Bakery is closed for the next two days. We help her clean up the shop so she's not overwhelmed after Christmas, and when she closes up at midnight, we help her clean up the cookies."

"She's open until midnight? That's nuts."

"It's fun," Bailey said. "I'm going to call you at 11:30, okay? You'd better come join us, at least for a bit."

I nodded. "Okay, if Momma is fine at midnight,

I'll come join you for a glass of eggnog and some cookies. Deal?"

"Perfect!" Bailey scratched Momma Cat behind the ears and left my room, closing my door behind her.

I could hear Jane and Rory run down the stairs and follow Bailey out of the house.

That's both the blessing and the curse of living in an old house like the one I lived in. You could hear where everyone else is at any given moment, thanks to the thin wooden floorboards and uninsulated walls.

"Looks like it's just you and me, Momma," I said to the cat.

My door pushed open, and Soot and Agnes came prodding in.

"Or not," I laughed.

It wasn't even late, but I could feel my eyelids growing heavy with sleep. Snowball fights were exhausting.

After spending some time with the cats, I laid down on my bed to rest my eyes for a short while. If anything happened to Momma, I should at least have been able to hear it and wake up to check on her.

Her weird mood lately worried me, and I wanted to keep an eye on her to make sure nothing happened.

I closed and locked the door to my room ensure she didn't quietly leave as I snoozed. Those cats had a habit of getting themselves into weird situations, and tonight I wanted to be sure to prevent that if I could.

I relaxed in my bed but found it difficult to sleep due to Momma's loud meowing. Soot and Agnes contributed to the cacophony as they joined in with Momma's howling.

However, sleep got the better of me eventually, and I dozed off to dreams of singing cats and snowball fights.

Something jolted me awake not too long later. I rubbed my eyes and noticed the dark sky outside my window.

I must have been asleep longer than I thought.

I'm not sure what woke me, but my heart was racing, and I felt an anxious knot in my stomach.

I checked my phone and saw that it was just after midnight. I yawned and pushed myself up, trying to focus my eyes through the darkness to find Momma Cat, who had grown suspiciously quiet.

"Happy Christmas Eve, Fat Momma," I mumbled through a yawn as I tried to focus my eyes in the dark room. I could feel Momma's warmth next to me on the bed.

I then sat up and froze as I sensed an additional presence in my bedroom.

Beside me, on the side of my bed, lay Momma Cat and a brand new little black kitten. The tiny new addition looked up at me and yawned, and Momma Cat purred into my sheets.

I slowly turned my attention from the kitten to the foot of my bed.

In front of me, just beyond my feet, stood two people staring down at me, their faces held expressions of both confusion and concern. The male form opened his mouth to speak.

"You're next," he said.

I screamed.

CHAPTER TWO

I sat frozen in place, staring up at the two spirits looking down at me.

The woman had a strange expression on her face. I couldn't quite tell if she was smiling or grimacing. The man had a look of concern on his face, and both crossed their arms and looked down at me in silence.

When my heart managed to slow, I finally found my voice. "I..." I couldn't come up with anything else to say, so I shut my mouth and stared back up at them.

Momma Cat and her new kitten didn't seem fazed by them. The new little kitten was curled up against Mommas' fur, and Momma was licking its head and purring.

"Thanks for the wake-up call, Momma," I muttered to the cat.

I turned my attention back to the two ghosts.

"Who are you?" I finally managed to say. They didn't look threatening, and I calmed down somewhat once I gathered my bearings of the situation. Spirits couldn't hurt people, so I had nothing to be afraid of apart from the clear invasion of privacy.

The two ghosts hovered in silence and didn't answer my question. The female looked to the man beside her, then looked back to me with a blank expression.

We stared at each other for a long moment before my phone rang and made me jump. Bailey's name flashed across the screen, and I answered and held the phone up to my ear.

"Happy Christmas Eve," Bailey shrieked into the phone.

I nodded into the phone, then realized she obviously couldn't see me. "Yeah," was all I said.

Bailey paused and waited for me to answer, but I didn't say anything else. I was preoccupied with the strange spirits in my room and could barely bring myself to speak.

"What's up?" Bailey asked. "What's going on?" She sounded worried, and I appreciated that I had a friend who didn't need me to overly explain myself every time something was wrong. She could often sense my emotions before even I did, and for that I was grateful. Especially now, and especially over the phone.

"You didn't fall asleep, did you?"

I laughed. That was the least of my problems right now.

"Uh, Bailey," I said. "Do you think you could come home for a bit?" The spirits watched me as I spoke into my phone, and I stared back up at them in silence.

"River, what's wrong?" The tone in Bailey's voice immediately changed. I could hear the laughter and music in the background grow quiet after she said it.

"Well," I began. "Momma Cat seemed to have had another kitten."

Bailey squealed through the speaker, and I had to pull the phone away from my ear. I could hear her announce the news to everyone else she was with, and excited squeals echoes through my phone.

When the excitement quieted, I managed to speak again. "And there are two ghosts at the foot of my bed."

Silence.

"Wait, what?" Bailey said.

I exhaled a deep sigh. "New kitten. New ghosts. Anyone able to come home for a little backup, here?"

"I'm on my way. Don't spook them." Bailey hung up, and I placed the phone on my bedside table for easy reach.

"Don't spook them," I repeated to myself quietly,

as I attempted a weak smile to the two ghosts in my room.

"So, uh," I said, scratching the back of my neck as I tried to think of a game plan. "Who did you say you were?"

After long minutes of more silent staring, I spoke again. "Really, you have to say something. You can't turn up in my room and not say anything."

The male ghost finally nodded. "I don't know."

He glanced to the female beside him who shrugged. "I don't know, either."

"Oh, well," I sighed. "That's super helpful, thanks."

I checked the time on my phone and hoped Bailey would hurry up. I twiddled my thumbs as I waited, sitting up awkwardly in bed avoiding eye contact with the spirits who seemed determined to stare down at me, unblinking.

Finally, after about fifteen minutes, I could hear Bailey running up the stairs and down the hall. She burst into my room, her hair disheveled and a worried look spread across her face.

"Are you okay?" she asked. She was heaving deep breaths, leaning against my doorway as she took in the scene. I saw her glance at the two spirits, but then her attention immediately turned to the cats on my bed.

"Oh my gosh, Momma look at you," she exclaimed as she ran over and jumped on my bed next to me. She scratched Momma Cat behind the ears and cooed over the new fuzzy baby. "Look what you did! No wonder you were so fat. I thought maybe you were stealing cookies, like River."

I rolled my eyes.

"Okay, more important matters at hand," I said, gesturing toward the two spirits at the foot of my bed.

"Right, yes," Bailey said. She sat up and turned toward the ghosts. "Who are you, and what are you doing in our house?"

When they didn't answer, I rolled my eyes. "Alright, so much for that." I crawled out of bed and put on a sweater to warm myself from the chill. The house we lived in was beautiful, albeit a little run-down, but the windows were drafty and now that the weather had cooled and snow had fallen, my room felt like an icebox.

"What are you doing?" the female ghost asked.

I laughed. "I'm cold, so I'm putting on a sweater. What are you doing?"

She stared back at me and didn't answer.

"Figured as much."

Bailey narrowed her eyes at me. "Do you recognize them at all? Any idea why they're here?"

I shook my head. "No, no idea."

"Have they said anything else?"

"Er..." I began. "Well, they said I was next."

Bailey's eyes went wide. "Next? As in, next to become a ghost?"

"Sounded like it. But seeing as they won't say anything else useful, maybe they meant I was next in line for the lottery. Or for a surprise. Or maybe they were going to sing me a Christmas carol."

"River, this is serious," Bailey chastised me as I began laughing to myself at the absurdity of it all.

"Yeah, I know it is," I said. "But, really, what the hell am I supposed to do?"

I turned to the two ghosts and waved my hands in front of their faces. "Yoo-hoo, anything else important to add?"

The woman looked worried. "You're next, that's all I know."

I sighed. "Next for what?"

She looked down at herself, all translucent and hovering above the ground. "For this. I'm sorry."

I blinked. "Wait, so you mean I'm actually next to die?"

She nodded solemnly.

"Oh, great. What a way to cheer me up just before the holidays."

Bailey held her hand over her mouth, and her eyes were wide with worry. "River, what are we going to do? We have to call Mrs. Brody. We have to inform the mayor and Sheriff Reese."

I sighed. "Because some strange ghosts seem to think I'm going to die? How do we know they're not joking, or confused? They don't even seem to know who they are."

"Do you remember anything else?" Bailey asked them.

Both spirits shook their heads.

"I'm sorry," the man said. "I don't remember anything, apart from the fact that River Halloway is next."

I blinked again. "You know my name?"

"Of course we do," the woman replied. "That's why we're here. To warn you."

I sighed. "This is fantastic. Merry Christmas to me."

Bailey immediately brought out her phone and began hammering away at the buttons, texting God-knows-who.

"Bailey, don't bother anyone else with this until we have the facts. It's Christmas Eve. Why don't we go back to Mrs. Pots' and celebrate, and we can figure this out later? No one will come for me if we're all together, I'm sure of it."

I wasn't nearly as frightened as Bailey seemed to look. Two ghosts appeared in my room, so what. They won't even remember who they are, so how can they be sure of what they're saying? The thought made sense to me, and I really wasn't worried.

"Let's go," I said a few moments later when Bailey ignored me and continued typing away on her phone.

I moved towards the door, but both ghosts immediately blocked my way. Well, in theory, anyway. I could easily have stepped around them or right through them, even, if I really wanted to.

"Please, don't," the woman said.

"We came to warn you. You're not safe. That's all we know," the man added. "Please, stay. It's not safe for you out there."

Momma Cat meowed loudly.

I glanced down to the cat then back to the ghosts. "So, what do you expect me to do, stay locked-up inside for the rest of my life? Who are you? Who's after me? I don't understand. Please, try and give me at least something to go on."

The ghosts shook their heads and held their silence.

"The gang is on their way back. Mrs. Pots is bringing the party to us. Let's go downstairs to Mrs. Brody's, and we'll all figure this out together."

I sighed. "Fine, but we're bringing the cats."

Momma Cat meowed again, and I walked over to scratch her ears. Her kitten was adorable and was all black with light blue eyes. The kitten was sleeping all curled up next to Momma.

"Where's Agnes? And Soot?" I asked, glancing around my room. I couldn't remember if I had locked them in with Momma Cat before I went to bed or not.

"Doesn't matter, let's get downstairs," Bailey said. "Mrs. Brody will know what to do."

Bailey carefully scooped up the newborn kitten and led the way downstairs. Momma followed closely behind, howling the whole way as she was very clearly unimpressed that someone was making her move.

The two ghosts followed as well, keeping their silence. I glanced back at them as we walked down the stairs to Mrs. Brody's basement apartment, and their faces gave away any number of emotions. Fear, worry, confusion, curiosity, to name a few. I had to admit, this was the last thing I expected to happen on Christmas Eve.

A crowd had gathered in Mrs. Brody's apartment, and I could smell the sweet scent of Mrs. Pots' baking as we came into the room.

Rory squealed at the sight of the kitten in Bailey's hand, and the two went to sit down in the corner of the living room by the warmth of the fire that Mrs. Brody was setting up. Momma Cat followed and curled up next to Bailey and the kitten. A loud meowing came from the back door, and Soot and Agnes came to join the crowd.

Four cats. We now had four cats. For someone who really never considered herself a cat person, I seemed to be becoming quite the crazy cat lady.

"There," Mrs. Brody announced as the fire began to roar behind the ornate fireplace. "That should keep up nice and toasty. Now, first thing's first. Who would like a rum and eggnog?" She was quite the sight, as per usual, with her messy blue hair and long brown nightgown. I'm not sure if she changed into it just now after getting home, or if she has been wearing it at Mrs. Pots' bakery. I wouldn't put it past her to do the latter.

I raised my eyebrow and glanced back and forth between the spirits and Mrs. Brody. "Really? That's what's first?"

"Of course, dear," Mrs. Brody said as she scurried into the kitchen. "We'll deal with your new friends in a moment."

I laughed. "Well, at least someone's got their priorities straight."

At least I wasn't the only one who didn't seem too concerned. The holidays can be a very stressful time for people, and the spirits were probably just lost and confused. That didn't explain how they knew my name, though. It didn't explain why they were in my bedroom to begin with, either.

I eyed the spirits wearily but sat on the couch and waited patiently for my eggnog before even attempting to explain the situation to everyone.

Jane and Mrs. Pots were chatting away on the other side of the room. Something to do with catering a New Year's Eve soccer party? Jane was really sporty and played for a few casual local sports groups. I suspected they spent more time socializing than actually playing any sports, though, from how tipsy Jane would seem after coming home late from her so-called games.

The room was warm and everyone had smiles on their faces. I couldn't help but smile as well. It had been a long time since I had a cozy family Christmas. Being a student in New York City was fun and all, but I did miss out on the holidays a lot. Everything seemed so nice and normal. Apart from the two spirits in the corner, that was.

I sighed loudly and accepted the large glass of eggnog from Mrs. Brody as she came back into the room with a floating tray of drinks.

"Oh, how lovely," Mrs. Pots beamed as the tray floated towards her. "How spectacular."

Mrs. Pots didn't have any magic of her own, but she was a good friend to us witches and had had magic in the family at one point. She was a good ally to have, and not just because of her endless supply of cookies.

The two ghosts observed in silence as everyone bustled about the room, cozying next to the fire, sipping on eggnog, and settling in the living room for a group chat.

Mrs. Brody set down the floating tray and went back into the kitchen to rummage through her cabinet.

The room was silent apart from the crackling of the fire and the soft meowing and purring of the cats next to the hearth. We all waited in silence for Mrs. Brody to return with whatever it was that she was searching for.

The girls watched the spirits as they stood near the door, fidgeting with their fingers and glancing nervously about. It was clear that they were both uneasy, and I really hoped we could get to the bottom of this soon. It was late, I was tired, Christmas was tomorrow, and I didn't want to spoil the holidays for the rest of the group.

Finally, Mrs. Brody returned with a large hardcover book and sat down in the large armchair next to the fire.

She cleared her throat and set the book down in front of her.

Finally, she smoothed out her nightgown on her lap and looked up at the two spirits with a stern look on her face.

"Alright, then. Who are you? Why are you here? And what do you want with our River?"

CHAPTER THREE

THE SPIRITS PACED THE ROOM FOR A WHILE, TRYING desperately to remember anything they could about who they were.

Mrs. Brody was flipping through her book, trying to find something that would help them remember.

This whole thing felt like an entire deja vu. Why was it that I was constantly having to help jog a ghost's memory? Since moving to Brimstone Bay this past summer, it seemed as if confused ghosts flocked to me at every chance they got.

This was different, though, as these ghosts were here for a purpose. They were here to warn me about my impending doom. Merry Christmas to me.

It was getting late, and we didn't seem to be getting anywhere. The only thing the ghosts remembered was that I was going to be next. They couldn't even remember how they knew, or who had killed them.

I yawned loudly as the clock above the mantle chimed 1 o'clock.

"We're not getting anywhere with this," I said. "Let's just go to bed and deal with it in the morning, okay?"

Mrs. Brody looked concerned but then nodded. "Fine. Sleep, then we'll get to the bottom of this first thing."

I sighed. "Alright, great."

"But you're all sleeping down here tonight," Mrs. Brody added. "So I can keep an eye on you lot."

I rolled my eyes.

"Seriously?" Rory complained. "But my bed upstairs is so comfy. It's calling to me!"

Mrs. Brody crossed her arms. "That's just too bad. If whoever did this to our guests is planning on finding our River next, then we all have to stick together."

"How many charms do you have placed on this house already?" I asked Mrs. Brody. "I doubt anyone would be able to come in even if they tried."

"We can't take any chances. Not until these two remember anything useful."

I sighed. "Alright, alright."

"Nancy, you better stay too, dear."

Mrs. Pots looked ecstatic. "Oh, how fun! I love a

good sleepover. It's been decades since I've had one."

I laughed at her enthusiasm. Leave it to Mrs. Pots to see the silver lining in any situation.

"At least we're well-stocked with goodies," Bailey said.

I looked over to the dining room table and noticed piles upon piles of cookies and cakes all scattered on top of each other.

"Wow, you really weren't kidding when you said you're cleaning out her Christmas supply," I said.

Bailey laughed. "It's tradition, every year we go and help. Isn't that right, Mrs. Pots?"

She beamed. "Absolutely. Wouldn't want these treats to go to waste, now, would we?"

Well, I couldn't say that it was shaping up to be a very normal Christmas. Not that I knew what one of those was, anyway. But, given our track record for weird things happening during holidays, I'd say we were just about on track.

I settled in on the couch and watched the spirits pace the room. They walked right past Mrs. Pots, who didn't seem to notice at all. She had always claimed to be able to speak with spirits, but it was becoming plainly clear that she over-exaggerated that statement. She had proven to be somewhat sensitive to them in the past, but then again, many people with any form of distant magic in their family line often had an affinity for the supernatural.

The spirits kept shifting their gazes back towards me, but I pretended to ignore them. Until they could offer me any more information, I wasn't going to give them the time of day. Or night. Whatever.

I must have dozed off because I was rudely jolted awake when the sound of a shattering plate echoed in from the kitchen. Soot had curled up on my lap but jumped off when he was interrupted by the noise.

"What was that?" I sat bolt upright, my heart beating heavily in my chest.

"I know who they are," Jane said. Apparently, she hadn't gone to sleep but furiously set about searching for clues on her laptop about the identity of our two spirits.

I ran over to her in the kitchen, and the rest of the room jostled awake, as well. Jane seemed to be the only one who hadn't fallen asleep.

I went to sit down next to her and yawned. "Don't you ever sleep?"

Jane shook her head. "Too much coffee. Look, here." She pointed at her screen, and I blinked through the fuzziness in my eyes after just having woken up.

There, staring right back at me from behind the laptop screen, were our two ghosts. Only, more solid and human-like.

"Oh, hey look! It's you, two," Bailey said as she joined us in the kitchen.

"Who are they?" I asked.

Mrs. Brody dutifully set about making coffee, while Mrs. Pots cleared room on the dining table for us all to sit around.

"Peter Darlington and Sarah Greene," Jane read out loud. "Missing from their homes in Portland since November 15th. No knowledge of their whereabouts, dead or alive."

Bailey whistled. "Dead. I guess we know that part, now."

I nudged Bailey with my elbow. "Don't be insensitive."

Bailey shrugged. "It's not as if anything we say will change the fact."

The spirits approached the table and were listening intently to our conversation. They kept looking at me with expressions of concern and fear on their faces, but they seemed easily distracted by Jane's discovery.

I looked up at the pair. "Peter Darlington and Sarah Greene. Do those names sound familiar?"

The woman nodded. "Yes, they do. I'm Sarah. This is my boyfriend, Peter." She smiled half-heartedly at him as he squeezed her in a one-armed hug.

I was mesmerized by their actions. I didn't know ghosts could interact like that. Maybe it had to do with who they were in life, or if they died together, perhaps.

That last thought made me pause. "Do you remember how you died?"

They both shook their heads.

I sighed. "Still nothing, hey? No more ideas about why I'm next then, either?"

They shook their heads again.

"Fantastic." I turned back to Jane who was clicking away at her computer. "Any more information about them?"

"No, nothing. Just a missing persons announcement. They haven't found the bodies yet, I guess."

I looked up at the two ghosts with sympathy. Their poor families must be worried sick. At least now, hopefully, we could give them closure. I would have to get in touch with the sheriff in the morning to let him know. He'd know what to do and who to call.

"Don't worry, we'll figure it out," Bailey smiled up at them. "River has a knack for solving crimes, apparently." She winked at me.

I rolled my eyes. So much for living the quiet life of a journalist in a small town. Murder and crime seemed to cling to me since moving to Brimstone Bay. Maybe I should try my luck in a new city.

Rory came to sit next to me and squeezed my hand. "Don't look so depressed. You've helped a lot of people since moving here. Let's see what we can do to help these guys, too, okay?"

I nodded. Of course, I'd try to help them. I was keen on helping myself first, though. There's not much you could do to a ghost, but there was plenty someone could do to me. Especially being the target of a potential murderer.

"We need to get more information. Have there been any other missing persons reports around here? Anything else you can find at all?" I watched Jane as she scrunched her face while she worked. Her fingers were flying on the keyboard, and after a few short minutes, she beamed back up at me.

"Yep. Two more. This time in Bangor."

"Bangor? That's really not far from here," Rory said.

Bailey smiled. "That's where Stephen King lives!"

I rolled my eyes. That girl had a strange obsession with his books. She had a poster of the murderous car Christine on her walls. I didn't quite understand the obsession.

"I've been there. It's spooky. I get why he writes the books he does," Jane shuddered.

"Okay, guys, back to the matter at hand," I said. I was more concerned with finding out how these guys were killed so we could make sure I didn't succumb to the same fate. Stephen King could wait. Although, secretly, I really wanted to go check out his house. But that could wait until later. Perhaps when I wasn't at risk of being murdered. Or, you know, summer time.

I shook my head to bring myself back to the task at hand. "Who are the missing people in Bangor?"

Jane scrolled down the website she was on until she found more information. "Jared Whitney and Sue McGowan."

I scratched my chin thoughtfully. "Another couple?"

Jane nodded.

"I wonder if there's any relation," I said.

Jane turned the laptop towards the spirits, and the woman bent down to look at the screen. Mrs. Pots moved to take some of the trays of cookies off the table to make more room for us all to see.

Sarah shook her head and scoffed. "Hardly. Look at them."

"Don't be rude, dear," Mrs. Pots said off-handedly as she busied herself with the trays.

I gaped at her, and the other girls looked back and forth at each other in mild surprise.

Did she just speak to the ghost? Mrs. Brody had insisted for ages that she could speak to spirits, despite not being magic herself. We always blew her off, considering her to be delusional, but maybe she wasn't lying this whole time, after all.

I raised my eyebrows as she stacked the trays on the counter. She didn't even seem to take notice.

Maybe she could speak to spirits after all.

"Huh." I was amused.

"There are more," Jane said.

My attention shot back to Jane after she spoke. She flipped through websites like nobody's business.

"Couples," she continued. "So many couples have gone missing along the East Coast. All around the same age range. None of them married."

She slid the laptop toward me when I reached out for it. She had tabbed the articles about the missing people, and I cycled through them. "You would make a great investigative journalist."

Jane laughed. "Sounds terribly boring."

I smiled. "Sometimes. Sometimes not."

I cycled through the websites again, taking note of each couple's faces. They all looked so young and happy, and they all looked so in love. What could possibly have happened to make them all disappear?

"None are from Brimstone Bay or the surrounding towns. Bangor is closest, but that's still about two hours away.

"How many couples are there?" Bailey asked.

I counted the open tabs on the screen. "At least twelve that Jane found."

"Yikes," Rory said. "That's awful."

I rubbed my eyes. I was tired, confused, and had absolutely no idea how any of this could possibly have anything to do with me.

I looked pleadingly up to the couple who were standing together near the table, watching us. They continued to look worried but hadn't spoken in a while. Maybe all we needed was to trigger their memories. I flipped back through the tabs to find the article that mentioned them.

"Sarah, Peter. Can you remember anything else about who you are? Where you're from, maybe? How you met?"

They both shook their heads.

"I remember we had to warn you. We know you're next," Sarah began. Her lip quivered, and her eyes looked sad. If she weren't a ghost, I would bet that her eyes would be welling up with tears as well. "We had to tell you."

"I know this is hard," I said. "But if your warning is going to be of any help to me, we're going to need more to go on."

"We're so sorry," Peter said. "I'm sorry we don't remember more."

We all sat around the table in silence for a moment, thinking. The fire crackled from the living room, and I could hear Momma Cat's thunderous purring from where I sat.

"What a sweet little cat," Sarah finally said. She walked - or floated, rather - over towards Momma and her new kitten. I wasn't too sure what to call it, the way spirits moved. They looked and moved like their human counterparts, and their legs walked when they went from one place to the next. But they sort of hovered over the floor like they weren't quite connected to the ground.

I watched as she bent down and looked closely at the cats.

Soot sauntered over to see what the fuss was about, clearly not wanting to get left out when any sort of attention was being paid to the other cats. Cats really were remarkable creatures, and they evidently had more of an affinity for spirits than Mrs. Pots did.

Well, at least up until earlier.

Soot sat down next to Sarah and pawed at a low-hanging ornament on Mrs. Brody's Christmas tree.

We all watched her watch the cat. She smiled, and Soot's shenanigans seemed to calm her. He pawed at the ornament and the surrounding tinsel until his claw caught the edge of the bow, and he managed to rip the ornament right off the branch. I laughed quietly to myself as he pounced on it and pawed it around on the floor.

"My cat used to do the same thing," she said quietly.

"That's nice." I blinked. "Oh. Wait, what?"

I turned to look at Rory beside me who stared back with wide eyes.

"You remember?" I asked.

I pushed myself up from the dining chair and walked over to her and the cats.

Sarah blinked up at me and frowned. "Sorry?

I smiled at her. "You remembered. You just said your cat did the same thing. Soot jogged your memory."

She looked back down at the cat and tilted her head to one side. "Oh. I guess you're right."

Mrs. Brody beamed as she made her way into the living room with a large glass of eggnog. I got a strong whiff of rum as the glass passed me.

"Sometimes, all it takes is a little bit of normalcy to bring back memories," she said softly. She placed her drink on the mantle and bent over to snatch the ornament back from Soot. The cat was none too impressed and stalked off grumpily when she managed to retrieve the red glittery ball from him. She hung it back up on the tree, higher this time.

Mrs. Brody turned to Sarah and crossed her arms. "Looks like all it might take to bring back your memories are a little bit of routine."

I sighed. "Yeah, but we have no idea what their routine is. How are we supposed to manage that without them remembering anything about who they are?"

Mrs. Brody motioned towards Sarah's necklace, which had a tiny cross hanging from it. "Well, it seems to me that these folks would likely celebrate Christmas, given the necklace she's wearing."

Sarah lifted her hand toward her collarbone where the necklace hung. She had a blank look in her eyes as if she were trying to remember something that wasn't quite there.

Bailey practically skipped into the room. She seemed ecstatic.

"What's going on?" I asked. "What am I missing?"

"Well, it just happens to be a certain time of year," Bailey said.

Mrs. Brody retrieved her eggnog from the mantle and cozied up next to the fire near Momma Cat and the new kitten. She gazed into the fire and let Bailey explain her epiphany to me.

"If normalcy will trigger their memory, then all we have to do is have a nice, traditional Christmas together. Chances are, if we do all the major holiday traditions, some of it is bound to bring back their memories."

Jane and Rory were both beaming wildly. Bailey clapped her hand in glee. I simply stared at them all, my eyebrows crinkled together and my arms crossed.

"So, you're saying..."

"We're locking ourselves in for the next few days to have the merriest of Christmases anyone has ever had."

I swallowed. "Oh, sure. Fun."

Christmas was never my favorite time of year. It wasn't even my tenth favorite time of year. Sure, I liked the lights and some of the music wasn't even too intolerable, but the idea of being locked in the house with a bunch of Christmas fanatics, a landlady who favored eggnog over water, a baker who insisted on fattening us up, and two lost ghosts seemed just enough to extinguish any hope I had of having a quiet and restful holiday.

"Well," I said. "Merry Christmas to us."

CHAPTER FOUR

I SAT ON THE FLOOR WITH MY BACK PRESSED against the far corner of the living room wall. Agnes sat on my lap and purred against my stomach as I stoked her fur.

The poor kitten was none too impressed that her mom gave her a new little brother. She was sitting in the corner with me, brooding, eager for the attention that Momma Cat was neglecting to give her.

Bailey, Jane, and Rory sat together at the kitchen table, compiling a list of every single Christmas tradition they could think of. From what I could tell from my little corner of the living room, the list had grown to be at least five pages long.

"You know, maybe we should just play some Christmas music. That might be enough to trigger their memories," I suggested.

The girls laughed at me and continued with their list-making.

I sighed and continued to pet little Agnes. I had a feeling it was going to be an eventful few days, so I figured I may as well conserve my energy while I could.

I heard talk of carol singing, baking, gift exchanges, among many other things being uttered from their lips. I had no idea how they expected to manage everything given the fact that we were locked up in Mrs. Brody's basement apartment for the next few days. She wasn't going to let us out due to the unknown danger that was looming over my head, so they wouldn't be able to go out shopping for anything new.

I doubted that would stop them, though. Not only were they crafty, but they were witches. If they couldn't find what they needed in the house, I bet they would find some way to magic it up. Bailey was a particularly clever witch, and I knew better than to underestimate her. All of them, actually.

I eyed Mrs. Brody who was busy rummaging through a box in the far corner of the kitchen. I knew not to underestimate that one the most. As small as she was, that woman packed a punch. I knew better than to get in her way when she had her mind set on something, and by the way her face was screwed up in concentration, I had a feeling she had made up her mind. Living in her house for six months had taught me not to get nosy.

So, I sat and watched. Sarah and Peter stood by and watched, as well. Every now and then they'd glance at me or toward the windows. I could tell they were waiting for something bad to happen, but they unfortunately just couldn't remember what it was.

I just wished this whole Christmas extravaganza thing would trigger their memories sooner than later. I didn't mind cozying up inside for the holidays, but somehow the knowledge that I wasn't allowed out made it harder to bear. I was trapped inside this warm, glittery, sugar cookie-smelling and Christmas music-filled apartment.

Life could be worse, I supposed.

My legs began cramping up, and I finally joined the girls in the kitchen. Their list had grown to about fifteen pages, and they didn't seem to be letting up anytime soon.

"Thorough," I mused. I pulled a few of the sheets towards me to take a look. I couldn't help the grin that spread across my face. They had even listed out every Christmas song they knew.

The clock above the mantle chimed, and I looked up to see that it was four o'clock.

"Okay, seriously," I said. "Can't you guys pick this up in the morning? I'm so tired."

Bailey barely looked up at me before returning to

her task of jotting down Christmas ideas. "Go to sleep, then."

I rolled my eyes and looked around the room. Mrs. Brody was still sorting through that box, and Mrs. Pots was snoozing near the fire. That left the cats and the ghosts. I decided to try and talk to the ghosts. Maybe I could get them to remember something without all this Christmas nonsense.

Peter looked at me with a curious expression on his face as I approached. Sarah was too preoccupied with the goings on in the room to even notice.

"How are you two holding up?" I asked as I took a seat on the arm of the couch near where they stood.

Peter shrugged. "Can't really say. Apart from you, I don't really know why we're here. I don't really know how I'm supposed to be feeling right now."

Sarah turned her attention to her partner. "Feel? Can we even feel anymore?"

Peter shrugged.

I still had a lot to learn about ghosts, and it seemed they did as well. It would really help move things along if they could remember more about themselves.

"Any new memories?" I asked. "Now that you've had a chance to settle in a bit, is there anything else that you can remember? Last place you guys were, perhaps?"

They both shook their heads and frowned.

I sighed and rubbed my temples. "Let's hope we can change that soon."

It was strange to me that they didn't remember anything. I knew that ghosts sometimes took a while to recall the events of their death and even memories of where they came from, but it seemed so strange that these two had absolutely nothing to go off on.

I remembered back to Jessica in October, a ghost I had found in a local haunted house. It took her some time, but she eventually did remember everything. She knew her name right away, as well. Then there were Mrs. And Mr. Littleton, and they seemed to have most of their memories. And Trey... Well, we couldn't find his ghost, so that was beside the point.

I sighed audibly. Something didn't seem quite right.

"Hey, Mrs. Brody," I called across the room.

The blue-haired woman looked up from behind the box and raised her eyebrows at me. "Yes, dear?"

"Isn't it strange that Sarah and Peter have absolutely no memories. Like, none at all? Does that suggest anything to you?"

She thought about it for a moment, then shrugged. "I suppose it is quite unusual. It could be due to some sort of magical influence, or extreme trauma?"

I looked the ghosts up and down. They didn't

seem battered or bruised. They were even dressed quite nicely. In fact, they looked completely healthy. Apart from their semi-translucent nature and odd way of floating just above the ground, of course.

Thinking back to the other ghosts I had met, they all carried their living scars with them as spirits. These two showed no sign of struggle or anything. I shuddered at the memory of young Jessica's back scars.

"You don't look like you suffered." I hoped that would at least bring comfort to them.

Sarah smiled. "Well, that's a relief. Wouldn't want to be stuck here as a spirit with no head or something."

I smiled back. At least she was trying to see the bright side of it all.

"Do you really think this will help us remember?" Peter was watching my housemates flip through their pages of notes. They were giggling, obviously excited to bring their plan to life.

I shrugged. "It won't hurt to try. The worst thing that will happen is we'll get some cheesy Christmas songs stuck in our heads."

"Well, that works for me. I love Christmas music. I think."

Peter smiled at Sarah and stepped closer to her. The way they looked at each other made me think they were new love. They seemed giddy together, and that tended to fade into a different kind of love the longer a couple was together.

"How long have you two been together?" I might as well give it a shot.

"Not long," Sarah giggled.

Peter blinked and I grinned. "There we go, another memory."

Both spirits looked at each other and beamed. I was happy that they at least had each other through this.

"Why did you come to warn me?" Worth another shot.

They both turned to look at me. Peter shrugged. "Not sure, sorry."

"Oh, well," I sighed. "Couldn't hurt to try."

"We'll get there," Mrs. Brody came to join us in the living room. She was carrying a small heavy-looking ornamental box in her hands, her fingers carefully wrapped around its edges protectively.

She pulled the small side table from beside the couch into the middle of the room and placed the box on the table.

"What's that?" I asked.

Mrs. Brody stared down at the box lovingly. Her eyes sparkled, and she smiled at it as if were her own child.

I cleared my throat when she didn't answer.

"You'll see," is all she said.

I narrowed my eyes as I thought I caught a glimpse of something move around the box.

I stepped closer to get a closer look, but Mrs. Brody held out her arm to stop me. "Don't get too close, dear. Don't want to compromise your inner Scrooge." She winked at me.

"I don't have an inner Scrooge," I countered. "I like Christmas just as much as the next person."

Bailey laughed. "Yeah, sure. So, you're not the one who has been hiding all of our Christmas CDs?"

I rolled my eyes. "I wasn't hiding them, I was simply replacing them with better options."

Sarah laughed, and I smiled back at her.

"Besides," I added. "Who uses CDs anymore? Get with the times."

It was Bailey's turn to roll her eyes. "Whatever, River. But now that it's actually Christmas Eve, you have no choice but to listen to our music selection."

I grinned mischievously. The CDs were upstairs in my room, carefully hidden in my sock drawer. There was no way Mrs. Brody would allow any of them to leave the safety of the basement. Not that Bailey would be able to find them, anyway.

"Okay, I promise. I'll listen to whatever you want," I grinned.

Bailey's face lit up. "I was hoping you would say that."

She reached into her purse and pulled out a

Celine Dion Christmas album with a red cover and waved it in the air in front of her.

My mouth fell open. "No! Where did you find that?"

I knew for a fact that was one of the CDs I had hidden in my room.

"You honestly think I only have one of these bad boys? I have at least three copies of this album."

I stepped back to the couch and slumped into the soft cushions. That was it, I was defeated. Christmas and my housemates would defeat me, and there was nothing I would do about it.

Bailey put the CD into Mrs. Brody's boombox. Yes, Mrs. Brody still had a boombox, let's not even go there.

The music started playing, but Bailey skipped ahead a few songs.

Suddenly the words "God Bless Us, Everyone" began booming through the apartment. I rolled my eyes.

"Aren't you atheist?" I called out loudly to Bailey through the loud music. She was already dancing and whipping her hair about.

"Agnostic," she called back.

The music jolted Mrs. Pots awake, but she seemed thrilled by it. She rubbed her eyes and stood up and began dancing with Bailey in the living room.

I laid back against the squishy cushions and

watched. Before long, Jane and Rory were up dancing, too. Mrs. Brody was sitting cross-legged on the floor, but she was doing some mad finger pointing to the beat, as well.

I watched them as if they were some strange alien race, completely detached and mesmerized by their behavior.

Bailey skipped over to me and grabbed my hand and attempted to pull me up.

"Not much of a dancer," I said.

"Don't care."

I grudgingly let her pull me up from the couch and into the middle of the living room. Mrs. Brody was carefully guarding the box with both arms on either side as she finger danced.

I finally gave in and began dancing, as well. Despite the highly religious words, I had to admit that the song was catchy. We danced and swayed around the living room, and then we all grabbed hands and formed a ring around Mrs. Brody and the box.

The two spirits watched us with wide eyes and amused expressions. I doubted this matched any sort of traditional Christmas activity they practiced, but you never knew. They could be just as deranged and outrageous as this bunch.

We danced in a ring around the box until the song finished, then we all collapsed in a fit of giggles. Even Mrs. Brody couldn't contain her laughter.

I wasn't sure if it was the eggnog or the sheer exhaustion, but no matter how hard I tried I just couldn't stop laughing. I couldn't stop smiling, either.

After a few moments of complete yet confusing joy, I eyed that strange little box of Mrs. Brody's again.

I did my best to collect myself and snatched it quickly off the table before she could stop me.

"What's in the box?" I demanded. The box felt warm, and I could feel happiness emanating from it. I paused and squeezed the lid shut. Strange, I'd never felt happiness ooze out of an inanimate object before.

"Mrs. Brody," I began. I held the box out and placed it carefully back on the table. I stepped back as she looked up at me in amusement. "What's in that thing?"

Mrs. Brody beamed and pushed herself up off the floor. "Well, I'm happy you asked me that, dear."

I raised my eyebrow expectantly. I had a feeling it was going to be good.

She stepped up to the box and lifted it with one hand, placing it carefully on one open palm. With her other hand, she lifted the lid.

We all watched in awe as swirling colors and lights overflowed from the brim. Music and smells and strange feelings came with it, too. It was as if every happy feeling I had ever felt from the holidays was condensed into one tiny box.

"No," I said. "Mrs. Brody. What did you do?"

She was beaming. Leave it to her to bottle up things that didn't need bottling up.

"Why, it's holiday spirit, of course."

"What?" I asked.

"How?" Jane added.

"Cool," Bailey said.

Rory simply smirked. She had been in the house the longest and must have already made this discovery.

"Holiday spirit," Mrs. Brody repeated. "Don't ask how or why. It's a long story. But it's simply wonderful, isn't it?"

I was about to ask another question but stopped myself before I got a word out. I simply stared at the small box of shimmery happiness. I had never seen anything like it in my life. Even growing up in a house of overactive and energetic witches as a kid.

I shook my head in awe. "It's amazing."

"It is!" Mrs. Brody looked out at us in reverence.

"I don't understand," Sarah said. She and Peter stepped forward, looking down into the small box in Mrs. Brody's hand.

The light from within was so bright, I didn't know how they were looking so closely. It must appear different to spirits, I supposed.

"If there's any time for this, it's now." Mrs. Brody held the box up for Sarah to get a closer look.

I smiled at her. She really was brilliant. I had no idea how she managed it, but I had a feeling that that might be just the thing to help our guests remember who they were.

"Now then," Mrs. Brody said. "Shall we get Christmas started?"

CHAPTER FIVE

THE CAROLING STARTED FIRST.

The girls sang their way through nearly every Christmas song they knew. They sang for hours, and we sat around the living room listening to them. Sometimes, when they forgot the words, we would have to play the songs on YouTube instead.

The sun rose and morning came, casting long shimmering shadows across the snowy back yard. Snow fell softly, and any trace of the mess we made by our snowball fight in the backyard was blanketed over. The house was peaceful, and I had to admit the Christmas carols weren't the worst way to ring in Christmas Eve.

It was much better than waking up to ghosts on your bed, that was for sure.

I sipped my coffee on the couch while the girls shuffled through their song selection. They seemed to have an endless amount of energy and barely stopped longer than they needed to eat a few of Mrs. Pots' cookies for breakfast.

I'd give them one thing - the girls knew how to sing. Mrs. Brody even chimed in for a few songs, but her voice rivaled that of a seagull, and she gave up after a time.

They paused again shortly for lunch, but besides the few moments we took to scarf down food, the singing continued. I could tell their voices were starting to get a bit hoarse, but still, they sang. I even joined in for a few songs after a while. Maybe the rum and eggnog I drank with lunch had something to do with it.

All rosy-cheeked and giddy, I sang at least four songs with the group before giving up and settling back in with the cats on the couch. Soot purred on my lap as I scratched him behind the ears. After the whole ordeal with Momma Cat and the new kitten, I figured he was happy for the attention.

It was about five o'clock in the evening when the singing finally triggered a memory.

"They played this song at your retirement party!" Sarah squealed after the girls began singing Mariah Carey's Baby Please Come Home.

Her sudden outburst startled me, and I spilled my eggnog all over my pants.

"You remember?" I asked.

Sarah was smiling at Peter, who looked as if he was regaining the memory as well.

"That's right. We danced to it." He said.

I did my best to wipe off whatever eggnog hadn't yet soaked into my pants and jumped off the couch. "That's amazing. It's working!"

The girls stopped singing and Bailey muted the music coming from Jane's laptop. She clapped and squealed in glee. "Oh, I knew it would!"

She was practically bouncing up and down, and I made a mental note to hide the cookies from her after this was all over. Too much sugar made for an overly excited Bailey.

"What can you tell us?" I asked. I watched the pair intently, waiting for them to say something.

Sarah screwed her face up in concentration. "Hmm, well I'm pretty sure it was a big party. I remember meeting lots of your ex-colleagues."

Peter nodded. "Yeah, that's right. The whole squad came out. It was a nice send-off."

I placed my glass on the table so as to not spill again, and settled back onto the couch. "Did you not know any of his colleagues before?"

Sarah shook her head. "No, we only just started dating a few months ago. I didn't have a chance to meet anyone before Peter retired."

A loud crash came from the kitchen that made me jump again. Good thing I put my drink down when I did.

"Sorry about that!" Mrs. Pots called from the kitchen pantry. The two older women were getting things ready for dinner. From the look on Mrs. Brody's face, she was not thrilled at all about having someone else fuss about in her kitchen. Whatever Mrs. Pots spilled in the pantry, Mrs. Brody was doing her best to clean up with magic.

"Out of the way, Nancy," I heard her grumble from the other room. "Move it or lose it."

Mrs. Pots squealed and jumped back out of the small pantry as a shimmery puff of white dust blew out from the behind the door. "Oh, my!"

I rolled my eyes and did my best to ignore those two. It was always best to stay out of Mrs. Brody's way, especially when she was in one of her moods. And by the way the pots and pans and cutlery and other things were flying around and crashing in the kitchen, I guessed she was in one of those moods just then.

"Wow, so I'm guessing you guys are all witches?" Peter asked.

"What makes you think that?" I grinned as the kettle flew out of Mrs. Pots' hands and onto the counter. "Ignore them. Let's get back to you guys."

"You look too young to be retired," Bailey offered. "What made you retire so young?"

Peter scratched his head for a moment and then shrugged. "I think it just got to be too much, you know? I can't remember exactly, but I think after working in the force for a few years, it just started taking its toll."

Sarah was running her hand up and down Peter's arm, and he smiled down at her. I could tell that they truly had strong feelings for each other. It was a shame they had so little time together alive. By the looks of it, though, they seemed to be getting on just fine together as spirits. I hoped that novelty wouldn't wear off after the holidays, for their sake.

"Peter just wanted a quiet life away from the city," Sarah beamed. "We were going to start a family. His work was just way too dangerous. I couldn't imagine how horrible it would be if we had kids and something bad happened to him. The stories he would tell me about the things he saw while on shift were enough to give me nightmares, sometimes."

"I can understand that. My boyfriend was a cop, and he made the same decision." I paused. "Apart from the whole kid thing," I added quickly.

Bailey rolled her eyes. She claimed I flaunted the term boyfriend too much, and always made a face whenever I said it. I did my best to ignore her. She was just jealous. Not that I could blame her, really. She had been having the worst luck when it came to relationships, lately.

Peter's memory seemed to have come back quite strongly. We sat in the living room listening to him tell stories of when he was a police officer for at least an hour. They still couldn't remember any further details about their murders, though, so we sat and listened patiently as he told his stories. I hoped that maybe one of his stories would maybe trigger a new memory.

Finally, after a long-winded story about a car chase and a traffic violation, Mrs. Brody came huffing into the kitchen all disheveled and hot tempered. "Dinner's ready. Come eat. Now."

The girls and I exchanged looks, then quietly obeyed and sat around the kitchen table. Sarah and Peter hung back in the living room, chatting quietly between themselves.

Mrs. Pots carried over a few really amazing-smelling dishes and placed them on the table.

"This is my famous yam casserole dish," she beamed as she placed a dish of steaming pink mashed yams in front of me.

Rory's eyes went wide, and I remembered her telling me about Mrs. Brody's candied yam dish. I guess Pots has won out over Brody in this round, and I figured that's what had made Mrs. Brody so pissy.

I couldn't help but laugh to myself over how ridiculous it seemed that we were locked in her basement because of the risk of my own murder, but she was preoccupied with being angry over yams. I shook my head and loaded a pile of the yams onto my plate. A small pile, as I didn't want to upset my landlady.

When Mrs. Brody brought out a giant roast turkey from the oven, we all oohed and awed over it. It was massive and golden brown and smelled like Thanksgiving to me. I wasn't used to this kind of meal at Christmas. I remembered staying in and watching Love Actually with a friend in New York last year. We ordered Chinese food and had a lazy day doing nothing. This certainly was a change.

"Oh wow, that looks amazing," Sarah said. She walked over to the table to inspect the spread. "What a fancy dinner."

Peter joined her, and both ghosts stood next to the table watching us serve ourselves.

I felt bad for them, as they would never be able to enjoy the taste of food again. Part of me felt too bad to eat in front of them, but another part of me was just so hungry. That part won.

I was halfway through chewing a massive bite of turkey leg when Sarah jumped back in fright.

"Oh my god, I remember," she said. She clasped her hands over her mouth and her eyes were wide with terror. "I remember something about the murder."

I nearly choked on the turkey as I tried to swallow the rest of my bite whole.

"What do you remember?" I wiped my hands with a napkin and turned my chair to look at her.

"The awards gala," she barely whispered.

Peter raised his eyebrow, but not a moment later realization dawned on his face, too. "Oh, yeah. I remember. The invitation."

Both ghosts stared at each other with fear in their eyes.

"What invitation?" I prompted.

After a long moment of silence, Peter spoke. "I was invited to an awards gala for members of the force. Sarah and I went. I remember getting dressed up for it and everything."

"What happened at the gala?" I asked.

Peter shook his head. "Nothing. That's all I remember."

"Well that's not really helpful, is it?" Mrs. Brody snapped.

Rory shushed her and topped up her eggnog with more rum.

"No, you don't understand," Peter said. We waited for him to finish, but he didn't.

Finally, Sarah spoke. "That's our last memory. The gala. It has something to do with our murder. We went, and then...nothing. Blackness. That's it."

My mouth fell open. "Did you die at the gala? Or on the way there?"

Sarah shrugged. "I don't remember."

I shivered and rubbed my arms for warmth. The room was hot from the fire and the food, but the thought of them nearly remembering their deaths made me feel cold.

The room was silent, and I looked up at the two spirits. They looked sad but didn't seem to be able to remember anything else.

Suddenly the lights went out, and I jumped in my seat.

"What the hell?" Rory asked. The basement was pitch black apart from the sparkling lights on the tree in the next room and the soft glow from the fire.

"Did the power go out?" I asked. I pushed myself out of the chair and walked over toward the front window. "The street lights are on."

"That doesn't make sense," Bailey said.

Mrs. Brody got up to find some candles and began lighting them around the room.

I shivered again. "I don't like the feeling of this, guys." I glanced about nervously, waiting for something to happen.

My body froze as I heard a muted thumping sound. I slowly backed up towards the kitchen table, my eyes darting between each window.

"What's that noise?" Rory asked.

Sarah began whimpering. "Oh no, it's happening. We were too late to warn you. It's happening."

Not that I would admit it to anyone, but I was scared witless. I glared daggers at Sarah for making the situation worse by her repeated mutterings of "she's going to die."

The sound turned into a scraping noise, and I listened carefully to try and place where it was coming from. After a moment, I realized it was coming from the door. Someone was trying to get inside.

I pointed to the door, and everyone looked towards where the sound was coming from. We all kept as quiet as we could and began walking together away from the door.

"It's locked, right?" Rory whispered.

Mrs. Brody nodded and stepped forward. She motioned for us to stay back with her hands, and she grabbed the broomstick that she kept leaning against the far wall in the kitchen. I wasn't sure what she thought she would accomplish with it, but I gave her credit for her bravery.

Mrs. Pots had her arms outstretched in front of Bailey and Rory, and Jane was standing with her fists in the air.

I couldn't decide if I wanted to run and hide behind my housemates, or if I wanted to go up and help Mrs. Brody. I decided I would go investigate the door so at least my lovely landlady wouldn't die trying to protect me.

My mind made the decision, but my body wouldn't follow. I was frozen in fear and couldn't bring myself to walk towards the door. I cursed myself under my breath for my weakness. I would never forgive myself if anything happened to anyone here because of me.

I finally managed to shake myself out of it and stepped forward to join Mrs. Brody in front of the door, grabbing the carving knife off the table on the way.

I jumped back and nearly screamed when the door shook and a loud bang sounded from the other side. I squeezed my eyes shut and took three deep breaths to steady myself.

Sarah was whimpering behind me, and I could hear Peter try and quiet her. She really wasn't helping anything. I tried my best to ignore her and started reciting the twelve days of Christmas in my head to drown her out.

When I finally opened my eyes, I took in a deep breath and stepped towards the door. I placed my left hand on the door handle and held the carving knife up with my right. I glanced back at my housemates and then to Mrs. Brody, who was standing strong beside me. She nodded to me and counted down from three.

On one, I twisted the doorknob and pulled the door open.

Everyone behind me screamed as a long shadow darted across the room.

"Oh my gosh, seriously!" I shouted.

I exhaled my breath and let out a nervous laugh.

I turned back towards the scared crowd behind

me and shook my head. "It was the damned cat."

Mrs. Brody looked amused then disappeared into the back room. The tension in the room eased and everyone began laughing.

"That doesn't explain the lights, though," Rory said.

"And lock that door!" Bailey exclaimed. "We're still not safe until we find the murderer."

Jane ran towards the door and closed it, then locked it and slid the small side table in front of it. I laughed at her, as the table really wouldn't stop anyone from coming through if they managed to break the lock.

She shrugged at me, obviously not caring. Whatever helped her sleep at night, I thought.

The lights came back on, and Mrs. Brody stepped back into the room. "The Christmas tree and the cooking must have blown a fuse," she said.

I sat down in my chair and held my hand over my heart.

"No more death scares tonight, okay?" I asked. "Can we just have a normal holiday, for once?"

Bailey laughed. "Fat chance of that happening."

The shadow darted across the floor again, and Soot came to join us in the Kitchen.

The cat meowed, and for a moment I tried to pretend that, for once, I could pass a normal holiday in this town without having to deal with someone dying.

CHAPTER SIX

I COULD BARELY MOVE AFTER STUFFING MYSELF with so much good food. It had been ages since I'd eaten a meal like that.

We used to make big turkey dinners for Thanksgiving when I was a kid, but that all stopped when I moved to New York. I attempted a turkey once in my small apartment in the city, but I ended up burning it to a crisp and ordered Indian instead. The gravy turned out okay, though, even if it was from a packet.

I ate it by the spoonful for a week. Don't judge me.

Jane put on some more Christmas music on her laptop, and we all lounged in the living room together to digest. Mrs. Brody brought out a bottle of port and poured each of us a small glass.

The tawny liquid warmed my blood instantly. I

wasn't used to drinking this much, and it was going straight to my head.

Now that everyone had settled and we knew we weren't being attacked by a monster through the door, we could spend some time to really get to the bottom of Sarah and Peter's mystery.

We didn't have much of a choice, given the fact that they were there to warn me about my impending murder. We either spent the night solving their murder, or I risked being murdered myself. I didn't much like that last option, so I did my best to concentrate and focus on the issue at hand.

"Do you remember who sent the invitation?" I asked finally as the ghosts settled in next to the Christmas tree.

Peter thought for a moment then shrugged. "No idea, I don't even know if I really paid attention to that."

I raised my eyebrow. What a typical guy thing to say. I kept my mouth shut, though, as I didn't want to come across as rude. By the expression on Sarah's face, I imagined his lack of "paying attention" was a bit of an issue between them.

"So, you just went to an event without knowing who invited you or knowing what it was?" Jane asked after I didn't say anything further. Her eyebrows were scrunched together, and she looked unbelievingly at him. "You just... went?"

He shrugged again. "There are always so many

events, I didn't even think about it. This one was honoring retired cops. Of course, I went. I remember really, really wanting to go, actually."

"Do you think someone knew you were going and was waiting for you there?" I asked. "Maybe someone who also got an invitation or who knew of the event some other way?"

"I don't know."

I sighed. My head was pounding, and I was starting to lose my patience a little bit.

"You must remember something else. Did you make it to the event? Do you remember anything after leaving your house?"

"He said he doesn't know," Sarah snapped. She was beginning to look frustrated as well.

I sighed. "I know, I'm sorry. You can't blame me for asking questions. You did come to warn me about my impending death, remember?"

Sarah looked down at her feet and mumbled an apology. "You're right. Sorry."

"We really are here to try and help you," Peter said. "I don't remember much, but for some reason I remembered your name. You were easy to find - your name is on every paper in town."

"And in most papers outside of town, too," Sarah added. "You were the one who wrote the piece about the murders here a while back. I remember reading it."

I nodded. "Yeah, I was." I had tried to block

those memories from my mind. It was never fun writing about people dying, especially not someone from your own town. And especially not when it was someone you knew.

"I still don't understand what I have to do with any of this," I said. Nothing was making sense and it seemed too random to really take seriously.

Bailey came to sit next to me on the couch. "We'll figure this out. With any luck, it will all have been a misunderstanding."

I nodded. She was probably right. "I hope so. It would be really nice to get out of the house. I'm starting to feel a little trapped."

Sarah sighed. "I'm so sorry. I wish we remembered more. Maybe if we do more to trigger our memories? The Christmas stuff seemed to work, let's do more of that."

As if on cue, Rory jumped up out of her seat with a huge smile spread across her face. "I know just the thing!"

She bounded out of the room before anyone could say anything and returned a moment later with a handful of Mrs. Brody's old, saggy socks. The pile of dull fabric hung from her hands as she waved them around excitedly.

"I'd be careful what you do with those, dear," Mrs. Brody said. She wiggled her own pink polka-dotted stockinged feet. "You don't know where those have been."

I stared incredulously at Mrs. Brody's wiggling feet, then looked pleadingly up to Rory. "Please tell me you're not doing what I think you're doing," I said.

"Stockings!" Jane exclaimed and jumped up to take some from Rory.

"You guys are nuts," I said as I shook my head. "And gross.

Mrs. Brody's socks were far from festive. Long and saggy with more holes than polka-dots.

Rory began handing them out to everyone and was met with looks of disgust.

I threw my hands up in surrender when she tried to hand one to me. "I'm not touching that thing."

"It's tradition to hang stockings on the fireplace for Santa Clause."

"Nope," I said. "That's gross. I'm not hanging any stinky socks over the fire."

Bailey laughed and rolled her eyes. "Don't be ridiculous, guys. Do you honestly think we don't have real stockings?"

She got up and walked towards the door that led upstairs. She glanced back to Mrs. Brody before opening the door. "Is it okay if I go up?"

Mrs. Brody nodded. "Bring back-up, just in case."

Mrs. Pots bounced up. "I'll go with you."

The two bounded up the stairs and disappeared,

only to return a moment later with armfuls of large red, white, and green things.

"Now these are stockings," I said as Bailey handed one to me.

I laughed as I inspected the thing. It appeared to be hand-made. I wouldn't expect anything less from our Bailey. Mine had my name written on it in gold glitter paint, with little silver bells sewn on. On the back, she had painted a cup of coffee and a bunch of cats. It put Mrs. Brody's gross old socks to shame.

Where she found the time to do this sort of thing, I had no idea.

We took turns laying the stockings in front of the fireplace. Jane had attempted to hang hers from the mantle, but the end caught fire from a spark and after an eventful few minutes with the fire extinguisher and Mrs. Brody's attempted help by flinging eggnog on the fire, we quickly decided to lay them on the ground, instead.

"Pass me your laptop," I said to Jane after the whole stocking fire fiasco had settled down.

Jane handed me her laptop, and I began reading more into the missing persons reports online. There had to be something linking them all together. It seemed too much of a coincidence that so many young couples went missing at the same time of year, all around the same areas. I doubted they were all just escaping the holidays.

I re-read through all the articles Jane had

open, and the girls continued singing carols in the living room. Sarah joined in with the singing, and apart from the strange looming feeling that someone was out there wanting to kill me, I was actually beginning to enjoy myself.

I tabbed back to the article about Peter and Sarah. Both were in their early thirties, outdoorsy, social, loved camping - or so the article claimed. There was no mention of anything that would suggest they would be the target of a murder. They were just two young adults who left town and didn't return.

I inputted their names into Google to see what other information I could dig up on them.

Peter's story seemed to check out. I found an old Facebook event about the retirement party they mentioned.

"Wow, two-hundred people RSVP'd to your retirement party on Facebook. You must have been popular," I said.

Peter laughed. "I grew up in three different small towns. Everyone had to show up, apparently. No one believed I was retiring so early."

"Three towns? Why so many?" I asked.

Peter shrugged. "My parents traveled a lot for work." He paused at the memory of his parents and looked down to his feet.

"I'm sorry," I said. It must be hard coming to

terms with your own death, I imagined. I really hoped I wouldn't have to find out first hand.

"Sarah, you were a gardener?" I changed the subject away from his parents.

Sarah beamed at me. "Yep! I was going to open my own nursery. I've loved plants my whole life. There's just something about nature that makes me so happy."

Her words seemed to have brightened Peter up. A wide smile spread across his face.

"Remember the time we went camping in Martha's Vinyard?" he asked.

Sarah laughed. "Yeah, and we got chased away by the person who owned the property. Turns out you're not supposed to set up a tent just anywhere."

"Just as well. Remember how wet and cold it was? We wouldn't have survived the night in that tent, anyway."

"Won't have to worry about being cold now, I guess." Sarah offered a partial smile and reached her hand out to Peter.

I was glad that they at least had each other as spirits. I wasn't quite sure how it worked, but I suspected they would be much happier lingering in this world together as a couple.

"It's great you guys are beginning to remember so much," I said. "Do you remember anything further about the night of your murders?"

They both quieted for a moment, and Peter

shrugged. "I'm sorry, nothing. But I'll keep trying. I think whatever it is you guys are all doing is working."

"I knew it would," Bailey sang from the middle of the room.

She, Rory, and Jane were dancing circles around each other to a 90's compilation Christmas CD. I thought I recognized Britney Spears. Not that I would admit that out loud, or anything.

I turned my attention back to the laptop and tried to see if there were any more missing persons reports that we may have missed before. Nothing new came up, but there were more articles posted about some of the ones we had found already. Letters from the families, pleading for any information anyone would offer.

We would have to let the sheriff know soon about the identities of the ghosts so he could contact their families. Their deaths would be the last thing they would want to hear on Christmas, and I wasn't sure if it would be best to inform them now, or after the holidays. Hopefully, their families just thought they had forgotten to call. On the other hand, if they knew for sure that they were missing, maybe the news would bring them some closure.

I read through one of the new articles I found on one of the other missing couples.

"James Shriver and Jerri Manson," I read the names of two of the missing people listed on the website I had open. I turned to Peter. "Do you recognize these names?"

Peter shook his head. "Should I?"

I skimmed through the rest of the article before answering. "He was a cop in a town half an hour from where you worked, apparently."

Peter shrugged. "Don't recognize the name."

James Shriver had retired three months ago, according to the article. He and his girlfriend had gone missing last weekend, and no one knows of their whereabouts. The family had issued a statement, begging them to come home. There was a video circulating online. I scrolled passed it, doing my best to distance myself as best I could. It was hard enough looking these two spirits in the eyes, knowing they were dead. I could hardly bring myself to look at the photos of the other missing people, knowing full well that they have likely met the same fate as Sarah and Peter.

I cycled through the other tabs. "Huh, this is interesting," I mumbled to myself as I read through the other articles. I hadn't caught it before, but there was definitely something linking them all together.

"Jessie Cardiff and Trevor Jackson?" I looked up at Peter.

He shook his head again. "Who are they?"

I turned the laptop screen towards them so they could see the picture. "Jessie is a retired cop as well. She's thirty-four. Retired this past summer."

Peter raised his eyebrow. "Another ex-cop?"

I nodded and turned the laptop back towards me. I listed off more names, but he didn't recognize any of them.

"There is one ex-cop in each couple," I finally said after thoroughly reading through each article at least two more times. "That's the link. That's what will help us figure this all out. There's no way that's a coincidence!"

The girls stopped singing and walked over to join me on the couch.

"Are you serious?" Jane asked.

I nodded. "Yeah, we need to report this to the sheriff right away."

I shut the laptop and tossed it on the couch beside me, then pushed myself up off the couch and looked around for my phone. I couldn't remember where I left it. I suddenly felt panicked as if I was running out of time.

"It's late on Christmas Eve," Rory said, reaching for my arm to pull me back to the couch. "He won't answer his phone. Best leave it until the morning."

"It'll be okay, Riv," Bailey said. "Relax. Nothing you can do about it just this second."

I sighed but finally nodded. "Yeah, you're right."

I fell back onto the couch and curled my knees under me.

"Anything else besides the cop thing?" Mrs. Brody asked from across the room. She and Mrs.

Pots had just finished a game of cards and were now interested in what was going on in the room again. She must have been listening, though. That woman never missed a beat.

"Nothing that I can find," I answered. I opened the laptop again and began looking through the missing people's Facebook profiles. Surprisingly, not many of them actually had Facebook. I guessed it wasn't the type of thing you necessarily wanted if you worked for the police. Privacy, and all that.

"I still don't understand how any of this has to do with me," I said. I yawned and stretched my arms up above my head. There wasn't much else to do but try and brainstorm, and I had a feeling it would be a long night.

I looked around the room at everyone else, but no one seemed to have anything to offer. We all sat in silence, deep in thought. Why would they come to warn me? What did I have to do with any of this?

I jumped as Sarah suddenly gasped.

We all looked up at her, and she stared down at me with wide eyes.

"What?" I asked. "Did you remember something about your murder?"

Finally, we were getting somewhere. I wasn't sure if I could pass another night not knowing my fate.

I slumped back when Sarah shook her head.

"No, but..." She paused and looked suddenly

scared. Her eyes made me uneasy, and I could feel it in my stomach that what she was about to say wasn't going to be good.

Finally, she blurted it out. "Didn't you say your boyfriend is a retired cop?"

CHAPTER SEVEN

"Take a breath, River," Bailey said.

I paced back and forth in the living room, dialing and re-dialing Jordan's number every time it went to voice mail.

"He's not answering," I said frantically. "What if they've already got him?" Tears were beginning to accumulate in the brim of my eyes, threatening to fall down my face.

"I'm sure he's absolutely fine," Jane said. "Besides, from what we found online, I doubt they'd take him without you."

I froze in place and stared at her. "Really?"

"That's really not helping, dear," Mrs. Brody chided. She was watching me pace around with an amused look on her face as if she were watching a strange new animal at the zoo or something. In situations like this, it was made clear that she obviously never had kids. Drama didn't sit well with her, and I kept an eye on her in case she felt the need to cast some sort of spell in my direction. She tended to do things like that when times got heated.

Once, she grew an orange on Rory's nose because her sneezing was distracting her from the New York Times crossword puzzle she was working on. It apparently took the girls the better part of the afternoon to figure out how to get rid of the thing.

I continued to pace. "Why isn't he answering his phone?"

The call went to voicemail again. "Answer your damned phone!" I shouted after his voicemail message sounded.

I then hung up and dialed again.

After a few moments, Bailey came and grabbed my phone from me. "Calling him again isn't going to help any."

I sat down in a nearby chair and buried my face in my hands. I felt defeated. There was nothing worse than not being in control of a bad situation. I was restless and couldn't sit still.

"I need to go find him!" I finally said as I looked pleadingly up at Mrs. Brody across the room. "Please."

Mrs. Brody looked to the ghosts who both wore concerned expressions on their faces, then back to me. She nodded. "Okay. Let's go."

I immediately jumped up out of my chair and grabbed my bag.

Mrs. Brody held up her hand to slow me down. "But we all go together."

"Fine," I said. "Good. Stick together, find Jordan. Yes."

My mind was racing a mile a minute, and I could barely maintain my composure. We needed to get to him fast before the killer did.

"Jane is right," Rory said as we all grabbed our coats and made our way to the door. "I doubt anything will happen to him. Every missing persons article reports they all disappeared together as a couple. He's alone, and you're here. I think that means he should be fine."

I nodded. Her logic made sense. "I hope you're right. I don't want to take a chance, though."

"I know," Bailey said. "Let's go." She led the way out the door and Mrs. Brody locked it behind us. We were quite the sight to see, a parade of witches marching down the driveway; some in Christmas attire, others in pajamas. Thankfully we had large enough hedges and a wide enough property to protect ourselves from onlookers on neighboring properties.

It was dark outside and a light snow fell from the sky. It was quiet, which normally made me a bit uneasy, having grown used to the city noise. However, the quietness eased my worries as I knew I would be able to hear anyone coming if we found ourselves suddenly under attack from whoever it was that killed Sarah and Peter.

Despite the quiet, I was on full alert as I led the group down the driveway with determined force.

We got to the end of the driveway, and I paused.

"Wait!" I held my hand out to stop everyone behind me. "We can't walk there, it's too far. He lives just outside of town. It would take us too long to get there by foot!"

Rory rolled her eyes. At least, it looked like she did through the darkness.

"Why don't we take my car?" Rory offered.

I furrowed my eyebrows at her, and then proceeded to count the numbers of our group out loud. Six. There were six of us.

"We won't be able to fit," I said.

I heard Jane laugh from behind Mrs. Brody. "You do know we're all witches, right?"

"Speak for yourself, dear," Mrs. Pots said in her kind, high-pitched voice. "Some of us are limited to magic in the kitchen, I'm afraid."

That woman always knew how to make light of any situation. I was glad she was with us.

I wouldn't be so glad if something happened, though. If I was going to be responsible for anyone getting hurt, I would never forgive myself.

I pushed that thought from my mind and focused on the matter at hand. We had to get to Jordan's house. We would be safe so long as we all stayed together as a group. At least, that's what I told myself.

Rory had a very small car, but she seemed confident in her offer. We all walked back down the driveway, and she unlocked her car for us.

"You sure this will work?" I asked, skeptical of what she thought we could manage.

"I'm sure," she answered from beyond the rolled-down window. "Get in, you witches."

Mrs. Pots climbed in the front seat, which left Rory, Bailey, Mrs. Brody, and myself to the back.

Her car was one of those really sporty small things, and the back seat really only fit two people comfortably. The middle seat was a small uncomfortable little lumpy thing that could maybe accommodate a small child on a good day.

Despite the setback, though, the other girls and Mrs. Brody climbed in through the back doors without worry. I reluctantly followed their lead and was amazed when I was met with a spacious area that accommodated all four of us in the back.

"How is this possible?" I asked. I gazed around the back seat of the car in wonder as I buckled my seat belt. We all sat comfortably next to each other, each with our own seat and seat belt with space to spare.

"The wonders of witchcraft," Mrs. Brody sang from the other side of the car. "No need to worry about it, dear. Just sit back, relax, and enjoy the ride."

I laughed and sank back into the seat. Sometimes I loved being a witch.

"Alright, Rory," Mrs. Brody said. "Hit it."

Rory pressed the button on the CD player, and we were met by more blaring Christmas music as she pulled out of the driveway and down the street towards Jordan's neighborhood.

Not five minutes had passed before we arrived at Jordan's place. He lived in a moderately-sized duplex at the edge of town, with a nice yard and an apple tree in the front. It wasn't really the sort of place I would expect someone like him to rent, but he seemed to enjoy it. He had a massive television and a comfy bed, so I definitely enjoyed it, too.

The lights were off, and I couldn't help but notice how eerily quiet it was as we approached the house.

I thought our place was quiet, but the constant crashing of the waves in the background provided a constant backdrop to the silence that I never really appreciated before.

This was quieter than any place had a right to be.

"Come on," I whispered. My voice carried louder than I had intended it to, and I looked around cautiously to see if anyone else could have heard.

The lights in all the houses were out, and we seemed to be the only ones outside. It was nearly midnight, after all. The kids and families would be all cozied up in bed waiting for Santa Clause to come bring them presents in the morning.

I, on the other hand, was waiting for a murderer to come and bring me death. Oh, how I wished I was a kid again.

I tiptoed up the steps to Jordan's front door and peered through the small window. There didn't seem to be anyone inside, but it was hard to see through the darkness.

"I'll try calling him again," I whispered to Bailey as she joined me near the front window.

I dialed his number again, and it went straight to voicemail. This time it didn't even ring.

I swore under my breath as I put my phone back in my pocket.

Bailey raised her eyebrows at me.

"His phone is off," I whispered to her.

I tried opening the front door but it was locked. I then knocked quietly and waited. No response. Finally, I rang his doorbell. I froze in place as I heard the faint echo of the ringing inside, but still no response.

"I don't think he's home," Bailey whispered to me.

I glanced back to the car where the rest of the group stood, waiting. I motioned to the side of his house and headed down the narrow path to the back door.

Jane came to join us, but Rory stayed behind with Mrs. Brody and Mrs. Pots. She had her phone out with 911 on speed dial in case anything happened. I really hoped it wouldn't come to that, but with my luck, who knew what would happen.

We reached the back door, and I tried the door knob. It was also locked.

"Damn," I said. "Everything is locked."

"Can't you just use your key?" Bailey asked.

I looked up at her with a confused expression. "I don't have a key."

Jane cocked her eyebrow. "Really? He hadn't given you a key, yet?"

"No, of course not," I snapped. "We've only been dating less than a few months. Why would I have a key?"

Jane shrugged and Bailey snickered.

I did my best not to feel self-conscious about the fact that I didn't have my own copy of his house keys, but by the amused expressions on their faces, I couldn't help but feel a little bit hurt. Should he have given me a key already?

I glared at them both then turned my attention back to the door.

"How're we going to get in?" I tried the doorknob again and gave the door a good strong shove.

"Well, definitely not by pushing it," Bailey snorted.

"What about the window?" Jane motioned towards the set of tall narrow windows above the back garden.

I walked over to try and open them, but they were also locked.

I raised my hands in surrender back to the girls, but Jane pointed up towards the windows high above me. "What about those ones?"

I looked up and shook my head. "No way. How do you expect me to get up there?"

"Very carefully," Bailey said.

Both girls came to join me near the back window. Jane got down on her hands and knees to form a sort of table for me to step on.

"You can't be serious?" I whispered to her.

She looked back up at me and shrugged a shoulder. "We can just go home then, I guess."

"Oh, shut up," I snapped. I grabbed Bailey's outstretched hand and carefully stepped up onto Jane's back with my soggy winter boots.

It took a moment to stabilize myself, but I could just reach the upper window.

To my relief, it slid open when I pushed on it.

"Success!" I smiled down at Bailey who gave me a thumb up with her free hand. "Now what?"

"You climb," Jane said from below. "And hurry, please. You're getting me all gross and muddy."

I stared wide-eyed at the window above me. There was no way I was going to make it up there.

"Hurry," Jane grunted.

I sighed and reached up to grab the bottom of the open window frame. It was either that or not know if Jordan was okay, so I figured I had no choice but to climb the damn wall.

I counted down from three in my mind, then clumsily tried to pull myself up through the window.

My first two attempts failed, and I hung down the wall like a limp piece of spaghetti.

The third time was successful, though, and I managed to climb up onto Jane and Bailey's shoulders for leverage. I very clumsily pulled myself through the window opening and crashed hard onto the floor in Jordan's back office.

I froze in place after the loud crashing noise I made. I was suddenly very aware that I was alone in a dark house that we suspected may be the site of a kidnapping. Or worse.

When I didn't hear anything around me, I slowly pushed myself up and poked my head out the window.

"You guys coming up, or what?" I smirked down at them. It was their turn to make fools of themselves.

"Nah, just let us in the door. We'll meet you around front."

I groaned. Of course, that made sense.

"Fine," I said down to them as they left the backyard to join the others at the front door.

I carefully closed the window and locked it with the little metal latch on the window sill. No murderer was going to climb his way into the house if I had anything to do with it.

When I was sure all the windows were locked, I took out my phone and turned on the flashlight so I could better see. I didn't want to turn the lights on in the house in case the murderer was watching from outside.

My skin crawled as I made my way to the stairs with the thought that the murderer could actually be in the house, too. I seriously doubted he would be, but the thought was still there.

"Jordan," I whispered loudly down the hallway. I peeked into his bedroom as I walked by, but there was no one there. All the rooms were empty, in fact. Where could he have gone? My heart was beating faster as I realized we weren't going to find him at home, after all.

I slowly made my way down the stairs, wielding my lit-up phone as a weapon. It wouldn't do much damaged, but it made me feel better none-the-less.

I reached the main floor and unlocked the front door and let the rest of the party in.

Bailey switched on the front light as she walked in, and I was blinded by the sudden brightness.

"Hey, what are you doing?" I shrieked. "Turn it off."

Bailey rolled her eyes. "We need light to see,

dummy. Besides, we'll be safer with the lights on. I doubt anyone will attack us in full light."

I sighed. Again, she was right. My mind must have been overly stressed, and I wasn't thinking straight.

When my eyes finally adjusted and my heart beat slowed down enough to breathe properly, we set about looking through the house for clues as to Jordan's whereabouts.

CHAPTER EIGHT

IT DIDN'T TAKE US LONG TO FIND WHAT WE WERE looking for.

The house was on a concrete slab foundation, so there was no creepy basement to search through, fortunately.

Not so fortunately, though, was that we found the item that I had so desperately hoped we wouldn't.

Folded on a small shelf near the kitchen table was an invitation. Or part of one, at least.

My hands shook as I picked it up, and my heart nearly stopped beating when I read what it said.

The invitation was for a gala dedicated to retired members of the police force, and the date of the event was Christmas day. Tomorrow.

I tried to say something out loud to let the others know what I had found, but my throat had gone dry, and I choked on my words.

My voice wheezed, and I began hyperventilating. I collapsed to the ground breathing so heavily that I couldn't get any words out.

Bailey and Mrs. Brody came running over to me to see what had happened, and Bailey snatched the invitation from my hand.

"You're invited to..." she read out loud. She turned the invitation over and gasped.

Mrs. Brody then took the piece of paper from Bailey's hands and read it through quietly to herself. "Oh, dear me," she whispered.

I immediately pulled my phone from my pocket and began dialing Jordan's number again. It kept going straight to his voicemail, but still I called. I knew the phone was off, of more likely the battery had died - probably because he was lying dead somewhere, alone. Still, though, I dialed. Every time I heard his voicemail message, my mind came up with some other horrific way for him to have been murdered.

I didn't realize it, but I had begun whimpering. Rory had run over to me and sat next to me on the floor, rubbing her hand in circles on my back.

"It's okay, River," she whispered in my ear. "We all know Jordan. There's no way he would go to something like that. He's too smart to fall for it. I'm sure he's just out with some friends."

I shook my head as I began to sob. Or at least, I tried to sob. No tears were coming out - I was completely dry. The thought of Jordan being gone completely seized me up.

"He wouldn't go to something lame like that without you, anyway," Bailey said. She tried her best to sound reassuring, but her voice wavered somewhat. I knew she was just trying to calm me down.

Jane, being the level-headed proactive person that she was, was already on the phone calling for help. She had dialed Sheriff Reese's number, but it went to his voicemail. She also tried the mayor, but his phone was turned off. On the second attempt at calling the sheriff, though, he picked up.

"Sheriff, It's Jane Summers," I heard Jane say into the phone. She held the phone away from her ear as I assumed the sheriff was giving her a stern word about calling so late on a holiday.

"Yes, I know. It's an emergency," she said. "We have reason to believe Jordan O'Riley may have been kidnapped. We're at his house now, and we need help."

I barely heard her tell him the address when the tears finally came. Hearing her say the words out loud had finally done it, and I broke down. I wasn't proud of myself, as I definitely wasn't the type of person to cry in front of others, but this was all too much. Jordan was gone. I might be next. It was too much for me to handle, and I buried my face in my hands and screamed my frustration into them.

It seemed like forever by the time Sheriff Reese arrived. He had brought two of his officers with him, and neither seemed all too pleased to be there.

"This had better be serious," he warned us as he stormed into the house.

I rubbed my eyes with my sleeve and joined him and his officers standing around the kitchen table.

His expression softened when he saw my face. It wasn't a pretty sight, I could be sure of that.

"I'm sorry we called you in on Christmas," I said. My voice was calmer than I expected, and it gave me a new sense of confidence.

I began explaining the whole situation to him, straining to remember every last detail. To his credit, he didn't even scoff at me or make a funny expression when I told him about the ghosts. He had never really believed the whole paranormal thing until I came to town in the summer, but he had caught on pretty quickly. His officers, on the other hand, had the expressions on their faces that you give to a child who was making up a ridiculous story. I ignored them.

"You're lucky you have a key to his place," he said to me as he looked around the room, analyzing his surroundings.

I blinked. "Uh, yeah. Good thing."

I figured it was best not to admit to law enforcement that I just broke into someone else's home.

"Is there anything else you can tell me? What else do you know?"

I tried to think if I had missed anything, and filled him in on every little detail I could think of. Apart from the lie about the key, of course.

I told him the identities of the two ghosts and their warning. I left nothing out. When I had finished telling them everything, with help from the girls for the bits that I left out, Sheriff Reese immediately got on his phone and began making some calls. He dialed number after number, filling in different people in difference jurisdictions with the information he had learned. Finally, he reached someone who was on Sarah and Peter's case and informed them of their likely deaths. He didn't mention the ghost thing, rather he said he received an anonymous tip.

"You should have brought this to me as soon as you made the connection between the missing people," he said to me while he was on hold with someone else, two phone calls later.

I shrugged. "Would you have stayed on the phone if it wasn't an emergency?" He narrowed his eyes at me then stepped away as a woman's voice sounded through his phone.

I paced back and forth while he was on the call. Finally, seemingly an eternity later, he hung up his phone and turned his attention back to me.

"Have you guys checked the restaurant?" he asked.

I paused. Oh, darn. "No, didn't even think of it," I admitted.

Sheriff Reese sighed. "Okay, well why don't you all go check Jordan's restaurant before we start panicking, okay?"

I nodded. "Right. Good idea." Wow, my brain really wasn't operating at full capacity. Jordan has recently purchased the local café and was turning it into a restaurant. He could easily be there now, working on the interior renovations or something.

One of the other officers pulled his keys out of his pocket and offered to drive us. Mrs. Brody and Mrs. Pots decided to stay with the sheriff in the house, and the girls and I followed the officer out to his car. I believed his name was Randy, but I couldn't remember for sure. He looked angry, and I wasn't going to be the one to strike up a conversation.

We sat in the car in silence as he drove us downtown to Jordan's restaurant. He had bought it a few months before when the cafe that used to be in its place shut down. The windows were still boarded up, though, as he hadn't found the time - or emotional strength - to hire a new pastry chef after his previous one was murdered. He also happened to be his best friend, so I didn't blame Jordan for taking his time.

The lights inside were off, but I knocked at the front door, anyway. No sounds came from inside, and it didn't seem like anyone was in there. I peered in the window through a small area where the plywood board had fallen. The place looked empty.

I knocked again, but no one answered. The sound of my knocking echoed in the silence until it faded into nothing and silence crept up once more.

I turned back to the officer and shrugged. "I don't think anyone is here."

The officer glared at me and stepped toward the door and rammed his fist loudly against the glass. "Anyone inside?" he shouted.

I jumped back at the loudness of his voice. It was a good thing there were no apartments on this block, as he would easily have woken people up with his shouting.

He glared again at me and got back in his car. "Let's go," he said.

I rolled my eyes but got back in the car as instructed. We drove back to the house in silence. On any other day, his attitude would have been enough to drive us all into a fit of giggles, but give the circumstance I just stared ahead and got lost in my thoughts. I tried to imagine Jordan going to some award gala and just couldn't picture it. It made no sense that he would go without me, to begin with, but even if he didn't want me to come with him, I figured he would at least let me know that he was going. At least, I hoped he would have. I thought we were close, but maybe I was mistaken. Maybe he went without me because he wants to break up with me. Maybe he doesn't like me anymore.

The car jolted as we drove over the end of a branch that had fallen on a side street. The sudden movement pulled me out of my dark thoughts, and I did my best to think clearly.

There was no way Jordan would go to an event like this without telling me, I knew that to be true. I convinced myself it was true.

The car had barely slowed to a stop in front of Jordan's house when I opened the door and jumped out. I ran up the stairs to join the others inside to see if they had any news.

Nothing had changed, and they all sat around Jordan's kitchen table waiting. Sheriff Reese had his phone on hand, ready to answer should anyone call with any information on Jordan's whereabouts.

As an ex-member of the force, I knew the sheriff cared about his well-being, but the worried expression on his face made me pause.

"What's going on?" I asked.

Sheriff Reese sighed and handed me an empty envelope.

I turned it around in my hands to inspect it, but it didn't seem like anything to me.

"What's this?"

"It's the envelope the invitation came in," the sheriff answered. "We found it in the trash."

"So?" I pulled up a chair and continued to inspect the rectangular paper envelope.

"So," the sheriff began. "There isn't an address on the invitation, and a piece is torn off, and it's not on the counter anywhere."

I peered into the envelope a third time. "There's nothing in here, either."

"Exactly." The sheriff looked at me with a heavy expression on his face.

"Well," I said, starting to sound frantic. "Where is it? Where is the address?"

Mrs. Brody shook her head. "We couldn't find one, dear."

"The person who sent it didn't send one?" I asked, hopefully.

Mrs. Brody shook her head.

I knew what it meant. I knew that it meant Jordan had probably put the address in his pocket. He was probably on his way there now. He was probably already gone.

I slumped back in my chair and felt the color drain from my face.

"You think he's gone," I said in a half whisper.

"I've made some calls," the sheriff said. "All towns where people have gone missing have been alerted. We have people investigating this, River.

The best we can do now is to wait here for more information."

I swallowed and nodded. I was no good at waiting.

Time went by slowly, and every minute that passed felt like we just losing time. I wanted to do something, but I didn't know what.

"We have to go search," I finally said two hours later. "We have to find him. We can't just sit here doing nothing while he's in danger."

I refused to sit put while Jordan was out there in danger. Whether he still wanted me as his girlfriend or not, I still wanted him and needed him to be safe. I didn't care if he wanted to go to the dumb event without me, I just wanted him to be alive.

Alive, I could at least chew him out for being such a stupid, uncaring ass. Dead, well... Dead is dead, and I had been around enough death in the previous few months that I really couldn't handle the thought of more. Especially if the dead person was my boyfriend.

"From what I understand," Sheriff Reese said, "you're in danger, too."

I shrugged. "I don't care. You have a gun, you can protect me. We have to go find Jordan. Please!"

"We have strict instructions from higher up that we have to stay here at his house."

"No," I said as I began to pace back and forth in the kitchen. "No. I can't. We have to go."

My heart was racing in my chest again, and I felt as if the ticking of the clock on the wall was getting louder as if it was mocking me. I glared at it but the second hand seemed to slow down even further in response.

Everyone watched me in silence as I pretty much had a meltdown walking in circles around the room, muttering things to myself.

The sudden sound of footsteps outside made me gasp and freeze in place.

"What was that?" Bailey whispered. She had nearly fallen asleep with her head on the table, but she snapped alert when I gasped.

I held my finger to my lips to signal her to keep quiet.

The sound came from outside the front door. My heart was going to beat right out of my chest if I didn't have a heart attack before hand. Sheriff Reese reached for his gun, and I stared unblinkingly at the front door.

That was it. That was exactly when I was going to die, I knew it. My skin prickled as I felt ice over my entire body.

The footsteps grew louder as the killer approached the front door.

I watched the handle turn, and the door slowly creaked open. I couldn't see past the door into the darkness beyond but a dark form slowly materialized, and I couldn't gain control of my legs to move back.

The door finally pushed open as Sheriff Reese raised his gun and shouted "put your hands where I can see them!" to the response of more male shouting.

I threw my body to the ground and covered my head, waiting for the sound of a gunshot or screaming or something. Anything.

Nothing came. My body shook in fear, but after a moment I raised my head to see what was going on. Why was it so quiet?

When my mind finally registered what I was seeing, by body collapsed again on the floor. This time, in relief.

Jordan was standing in the front door with his arms in the air and an extremely confused and angry expression on his face.

CHAPTER NINE

"Can someone please tell me what you're all doing here?" Jordan asked as he stepped into his kitchen.

"I..." I started, but couldn't think of what to say. I was just so happy to see that man's face. I pushed myself up off the ground and lunged at him, wrapping my arms around him and burying my face into his neck.

Normally I wasn't one for PDA, but at that moment I really didn't care.

"I thought you were dead," I said into his neck.

He softly pushed me partially off of himself so he could look me in the eye. I shrugged sheepishly and kissed him.

"Can you point that thing somewhere else?" he growled at Sheriff Reese.

The sheriff slid the gun back into its holster and

relaxed his stance. "Glad to see you're alright," he finally said.

Jordan raised his eyebrow. "Anyone going to fill me in?"

I shook my head dramatically, and to my dismay, my eyes began to fill with tears again. "No. First, you tell us where the hell you have been! I've been calling you for hours."

I slammed my fists against his chest. I had so many emotions rushing through me, I didn't know whether I was relieved, angry, happy, or what. I didn't know how to express myself, so I continued to hit him until he grabbed my hands with his and led me to a chair in the kitchen and sat me down.

"I'll make tea," Mrs. Pots said. She got up and began scurrying about in the kitchen looking for a teapot.

I had nearly forgotten she was with us, this was the first she'd spoken anything since we'd left the house.

Jordan watched her with an amused look on his face but didn't offer any guidance on where to find the teapot.

I highly doubted he owned one.

"So, where were you?" I repeated once I had calmed down a bit.

He scrunched his eyebrows together, and I couldn't tell if he was angry or amused.

"I was fishing," he finally said.

I jumped out of my chair. "Are you kidding me? Why the hell would you go fishing at night? And on Christmas Eve? That makes absolutely no sense!"

"Relax, River," he said. He pushed down on my shoulders until I sat back down in the chair.

I glared at him. That man had absolutely no idea what awful hell he had put me through over the previous few hours.

"Brett and I went ice fishing up north," he clarified. "We stopped for a late dinner on the drive back, and we took our time because the roads were icy."

I blew out a loud sigh. "Brett? Ryan's friend?"

Jordan nodded. "Yeah, he's my friend, too. I knew you were busy with your Christmas stuff, so I agreed to go on a guy's fishing trip with him."

I gaped at him. From what I remembered from meeting Brett a few months back, he was a complete jackass. I couldn't imagine what the two of them had in common.

"Are you going to tell me what you're all doing in my house?" he asked the room.

Everyone looked back and forth amongst themselves sheepishly.

The sheriff and his men were the only ones who didn't look embarrassed, but then again, they didn't know we had broken into Jordan's home.

I sighed and rubbed my eyes, trying to come up with a clear way to explain what was going on.

"Two ghosts appeared on my bed this morning and told me I was next to die," I finally said. Might as well have started from the beginning.

He stared at me, and his mouth fell open. "Come again?"

I proceeded to tell him the whole story, from when the ghosts first appeared to our breaking into his house.

Sheriff Reese did not look impressed when I admitted that last part, but to his credit he kept his mouth shut and let me finish the story.

"I don't understand," Jordan said, finally. "Why would they be after ex-cops and their girlfriends?"

I shook my head. "I have no idea, but whatever the reason, we're not safe."

Sheriff Reese's phone buzzed, but he swiped it to ignore the call. "Do you have the rest of the invitation?" he asked Jordan.

"The what?"

"The invitation to the gala," the sheriff said.

"Oh. Yeah, maybe." Jordan patted his jacket pockets and looked around himself on the floor. "Damn, I left my bag with Brett."

"The invitation is in the bag?" Sheriff Reese asked.

"Yeah, is it important?"

I nodded. "Very. It could be the clue we need to find out more about who is doing this, and why."

"I'll call Brett. He shouldn't be too far, it won't

be a problem for him to bring it back." Jordan pulled his phone from his jacket pocket and began texting his friend.

I rolled my eyes. Great, now I would have to see that jerk again. That guy left a bad taste in my mouth.

"Better get him to bring it to their house," the sheriff nodded towards me. "I'd like you all to stay together tonight, for your own safety. I don't think it's a good idea for you to be here, given the fact that whoever is drawing the missing people away knows your address."

Jordan nodded. "Sure thing."

When Jordan's phone didn't buzz back, he dialed his friend's number and went into the other room to talk. I heard him leave a quick message, though, and he returned a few seconds later.

"Voicemail," he said. "Hopefully he gets it before getting all the way home."

I sighed. "Well, no sense waiting around here. Let's get going."

"I'll drive," Jordan said.

"Rory's got her car, but I'll go with you," I said.

The sheriff grabbed his jacket and keys from the kitchen table. "Works for me. You guys stay safe. I'll go make some more calls and we'll arrange to go investigate the event site in the morning when there's light."

I nodded. "Good idea. Do you remember if it was far?" I asked Jordan.

Jordan shook his head. "Less than an hour away, I think. I can't remember the exact address, but it was just a town or two over."

"Well, hopefully, your friend gets back to you soon. If he can't return the bag, ask him for the address on your invitation," Sheriff Reese said as he shook Jordan's hand. "Stay safe. We'll be in touch tomorrow."

We all followed the sheriff and his officers out of the house, and Jordan locked up behind us.

I went ahead and took a seat in his car as the rest of my group piled into Rory's car, and I watched the girls drive away in front of us as Jordan joined me in his.

We drove in silence for a minute while I tried my very best to keep my cool, but my mind wasn't having any of it at that moment.

"What the hell did you think you were doing going out fishing in the middle of the night?" I basically shouted at him as he drove.

Jordan jumped at my sudden outburst and pulled the car over. He looked me level in the eye and spoke calmly. "River, we didn't go at night. We went early this morning. I told you, the roads were bad and we took our time to get home."

"I thought you had gone to the gala," I finally

said after staring out the window, avoiding his eye contact.

"The gala?" he asked. "Oh, the invitation. Why would you think I would go to something like that without you?"

I really didn't want to admit to him that the thought of him not wanting to be with me with me scared me more than the idea of both of us being kidnapped. I knew how ridiculous it sounded, so I kept it to myself. I didn't want to scare the poor boy off.

"Did you want to go?" I asked.

Jordan considered for a moment. "Well, I was really planning on it. I wanted to go so bad, for some reason."

I nodded. "Makes sense. It's nice to be honored for your work."

"But," Jordan continued, "now that I look back on it, I really couldn't care less if I go. I'm really not the gala type of guy."

I turned back towards him and glanced down at his torn jeans and leather jacket. "Yeah, you don't really strike me as the suit and tie kind of guy."

He grinned at me. "And you don't strike me as the ball gown type of girl."

I laughed. "Definitely not. Besides, who said I even wanted to go with you?"

Jordan rolled his eyes. "Oh, come on. You know how irresistible I'd look in a tux. You wouldn't be able to stay away." He winked at me, and it was my turn to roll my eyes.

"Whatever you say, Danny." We had watched Greece a few weeks ago, and I liked to tease him about how much he dressed like him. All he needed was the black hair, and he'd be all set.

"I was seriously considering going," he said. "But Brett called and wanted to go fishing, so I decided to go with him. The gala wasn't until tomorrow, anyway. I couldn't stop thinking about the damn gala, though, when we were away."

I shrugged but said nothing. I still couldn't believe that he was out fishing when I honestly thought he was dead. I could sense another outburst coming. I wasn't particularly emotionally stable, apparently.

Oh, and there it came. "I thought you were dead! You weren't answering your phone!" My breathing quickened as another bout of anxiety came on. "You went fishing, and I thought you had been kidnapped and murdered."

Jordan placed his hands on my shoulders to calm me down. "River, it's okay. I'm okay, everyone's okay. You can't let yourself get worked up about something that could have happened. If what you guys have told me is right, we have to focus our energy on the future to make sure no one else gets hurt."

I nodded. He was right, of course. He always was.

"Yeah, I know," I sighed. "You just have no idea what I've been going through the last few hours."

"I'm sorry." Jordan pulled back onto the street and continued to drive towards my house. Luckily Brimstone Bay was a fairly small town, and we didn't live too far from one another.

"How did you get into my house, anyway?" Jordan laughed.

I scrunched my face, trying to come up with some better explanation that avoided the whole breaking in thing. Unfortunately, I couldn't come up with anything clever.

"Window," I muttered. I looked down at my feet and realized I was still wearing my slippers. In the mad panic of leaving the house to find Jordan earlier on, I totally forgot to put on my boots.

"All the lower winders were locked," Jordan answered. He looked amused.

I was glad at least someone was having a good time. I rolled my eyes.

"Upper window," I muttered again.

Jordan laughed. "You mean you climbed up through the upstairs window? I would have loved to have seen that."

"It wasn't a particularly graceful experience," I commented.

Jordan shook his head and laughed. "You're

probably the clumsiest person I know. I can only imagine what you would have looked like climbing up the side of my house."

I glowered. "Whatever. Just drive."

He reached his arm around me and squeezed my shoulder. "Relax, River. We're all together. We're all okay. Everything will be okay."

I hoped he was right.

A few minutes later, Jordan pulled his car up my driveway and parked right behind Rory's. He walked around to the passenger side and took my hand as we walked into the house together.

My mood instantly lifted when I saw the look on his face as we walked into Mrs. Brody's apartment.

"It looks like Christmas threw up in here," he said. His eyes were darting from the Christmas tree to the massive pile of cookies on the table, then back again to the Christmas tree and the stockings lying out in front of the fire.

His eyes lingered on the pile of Mrs. Brody's old socks that were still out, but to his credit he didn't even question it. He had gotten to know us all pretty well over the past few months, and he had grown to expect strange things.

"I know, it's a bit much," I said. "But there's a method to our madness."

Jordan took off his snowy boots, but as I was already in my slippers, so I just dried them off on the mat and then led Jordan to the couch.

"We're trying to jog the ghosts' memories," Rory said.

She came to join us and sat down cross-legged on the floor near the fire.

"Where are the ghosts now?" Jordan asked.

I glanced around the room but didn't see any sight of them. Mrs. Brody and Mrs. Pots were busy working away in the kitchen, organizing preparations for breakfast for something, by the looks of it. Jane and Bailey were at the kitchen table, helping out by eating the cookies. Sarah and Peter, though, weren't anywhere to be seen.

"I'm not sure. They're not here at the moment."

Jordan nodded and seemed to relax a bit, which made me smirk. "Uncomfortable around ghosts?"

He shrugged. "Don't know, never been around them before."

I thought back to the many times he'd come over to the house where Mrs. Brody's spirit friends were hanging around as well. I kept my mouth shut, though, as I didn't want to upset him. It must be strange knowing there's another entity in the same room as you and not being able to see or sense them.

"So, how exactly is Christmas stuff supposed to jog their memories?"

Rory began explaining our whole theory behind the tradition and memory thing as Mrs. Brody brought over a tray of eggnog and cookies. I grabbed a large mug and moaned into it as I sipped the thick, sweet rum-filled drink. Mrs. Brody knew exactly what I needed, and I sat there in silence sipping from the mug as Rory carried on with her story.

Jordan tried to politely pass on the eggnog, but Mrs. Brody insisted and placed a mug in front of him as well.

"We should all get some sleep," I yawned. "At least a few hours before tomorrow."

"Oh!" Bailey bounded into the living room with her arms in the air, signaling for me to wait. "Hold on, I've got one for you, too!" She beamed at Jordan, then ran from the room and through the door leading upstairs.

Jordan stared after her with his eyebrow raised, but Rory and I knew exactly what she was up to.

A moment later, she bounded back into the room carrying an exceptionally massive green stocking, complete with sewn on silvery garland and the name 'Jordan' spelled across the front in red paint.

"Here," Bailey said. "Add it to ours in front of the fire before we all go to bed."

A smile spread across Jordan's face as she tossed him the stocking.

I watched as he added his enormous stocking to the collection on the floor, and couldn't help but smile.

"Welcome to the family."

CHAPTER TEN

Mrs. Brody allowed Jordan and I to sleep up in my room, given that there really wasn't much room on the floor in her place. I supposed having an ex-cop as a boyfriend had its advantages.

Well, apart from the whole ex-cop missing person thing.

We were woken up not long falling asleep, it seemed, by banging noises coming up from below the floor, and I could faintly hear Bailey's voice coming through the floorboards shouting that breakfast was ready.

I yawned and stretched and reluctantly rolled out of bed and put a new pair of slippers on. My favorite ones I wore last night got pretty filthy wearing then out of the house like I did. Idiot.

I smiled down at Jordan who could barely open

his eyes. This was the first time that he had spent the night.

Not that anything had happened, mind you. But it was nice seeing how comfortable he was staying over. It made my worrying about him wanting to break up with me and go to the gala without me seem like such a stupid thing.

"Come on," I said as I reached for his hand. "Breakfast is ready, and we don't want to keep the girls waiting."

I tried to pull his arm, but he was stronger, and he managed to pull me back into bed. He kissed me and then playfully pushed me off the bed.

"Yeah, yeah," he said. "Can I shower first?"

I shrugged. "If you must. I'll be downstairs. There's a coffee with my name on it, and I don't want to keep it waiting."

I rummaged through my closet and found a spare towel and threw it on him as I left the room. "Don't take too long," I called back to him.

"I won't," he laughed.

I paused and turned at the door. "And don't sneak away for any galas or anything, okay?"

He winked at me, and I grinned. "Go get your coffee. I'll be down in a few minutes."

I left him to his privacy and went down to join the girls downstairs. Mrs. Brody was furiously working away in the kitchen, flipping pancakes and poking at the sausages on the stove.

I immediately walked up to the counter and poured myself a large mug of hot coffee before joining the girls at the kitchen table.

"Merry Christmas," Rory beamed.

"Merry Christmas," I replied.

Everyone else in the room repeated the words as well.

I glanced around. "Where'd Mrs. Pots go?"

Mrs. Brody spoke without even taking a moment's pause from her work. "She left an hour ago. Going to her sister's for Christmas day to spend time with her nephew."

"Mrs. Brody let her leave, given the fact that we know she's not in any danger," Bailey smirked.

"You, on the other hand," Jane said, "aren't leaving our sight."

I sipped my coffee and smiled. "I've got nowhere to go just yet, so I'm all yours."

I looked around the room and noticed even more decorations has been strung up. "When the heck did you find the time to do this?"

Bailey laughed. "There are twenty-four usable hours in every day!"

I rolled my eyes. "Yes, but many of those are meant for sleeping. You do know that, right?"

"Not at Christmas," Bailey scoffed. "Can't be wasting any precious time!"

Bailey was positively radiant, and there wasn't a dark circle under her eyes or anything. I had no idea how she did it, but that girl really was Wonder Woman.

I admired her work, then nearly jumped in my seat as I noticed Sarah and Peter standing around the Christmas tree.

"Oh, hello!" I called to them. "Merry Christmas."

Sarah beamed back at me and waved. "Merry Christmas! We were just admiring your ornaments. How did you manage to make them change like this?"

I wasn't sure what she was talking about, so I went to join them by the tree to look.

The hanging ball ornaments had photographs of us on them, and each one changed or moved as you looked at it. There was one of Mrs. Brody, back when she had pink hair, on an ornament near the bottom that waved up at me when I looked at it. I reluctantly waved back, then glanced over toward Mrs. Brody in the kitchen.

She took no notice, and I figured the ornaments must have been spelled.

Bailey joined us and had a massive grin spread across her face. "Like it?" she asked. "I came up with the idea last night."

I couldn't help but laugh. "I think you may have had too much eggnog."

I lifted an ornament with an image of Soot on it, and the cat in the photograph was trying to paw the next ornament over. Luckily, he couldn't reach and was restricted to the surface of the decoration he was painted on.

"Where are the cats, anyway?" I asked.

"Getting into trouble somewhere, I'd imagine," Bailey said.

Jordan came down the stairs just then, and we all turned towards him as he stepped into the room.

"Merry Christmas," all the girls shouted at him at once.

He laughed cheerfully and wished them all a Merry Christmas in turn.

He came to join us at the Christmas tree, and I showed him the ornaments Bailey had made. The look on his face made me laugh. He looked like a small child meeting Santa for the first time. The wonder and amazement in his eyes warmed my heart, and I couldn't help but pull him in for a tight hug.

"This is incredible," he said into my hair.

I squeezed him then pushed him away so I could look at him. "Oh, you haven't seen anything, yet."

He raised his eyebrow, but before I could warn him about what sort of Christmas craziness my housemates were capable of, Mrs. Brody called us into the kitchen for breakfast.

The cookies had mostly been put away, apart from some amazing looking chocolate balls that Rory insisted were a necessary part of Christmas breakfast. Trays of sausage, pancakes, bagels, and a whole ton of other strange things were scattered across the table. It was enough food to feed the entire neighborhood.

Just as we sat down, the cats paraded into the room. I grinned at Soot as he came and sat on the floor at my feet. He could smell the food, the little brat.

"You only love me for my food," I said to him as I scratched his ears. He purred into my hand, and I 'accidentally' dropped a piece of sausage on the floor for him to eat. He chomped into it with his mouth and padded away towards the fireplace, where he settled down to eat it. That cat really seemed more like a dog, at times. No wonder I was so fond of him.

When I turned my attention back to the table after watching Soot, I nearly spat out my coffee.

Everyone else was maintaining a straight face, focusing on their breakfasts, but I couldn't help but stare. Jordan's hair had gone from a light sandy blond to a bright Red with streaks of green.

He raised his eyebrows at me as I gaped at him, but I pursed my lips together to refrain from laughing as Jane kicked my leg from under the table.

"What are you looking at?" Jordan asked.

I shook my head and shrugged. "Nothing, sorry. Just thought I saw a ghost."

Jordan immediately looked behind himself to

check, not that he would have been able to see a ghost anyway. I kept Sarah and Peter's presence quiet from him, so as to not make him uneasy. But he would have to learn to get used to it, eventually.

I piled a bunch of food onto my plate and began to eat, but after taking a bite of pancake, I nearly spat that out from laughing as well.

Jordan's eyebrows had turned green, and they sparkled as if bits of silver garland were woven into them.

"What?" Jordan insisted. "What's wrong with you?"

I raised my coffee mug to my lips to hide the grin I couldn't control. "Nothing, nothing," I said.

Jordan rolled his eyes and gave me a strange look. "Maybe you should go back to sleep."

I shook my head. "No, I'm fine. Just need more coffee."

I sipped my coffee and noticed Mrs. Brody's face was all scrunched up in concentration. Uh oh, that was never a good sign.

Bailey was barely holding back laughter at the other end of the table, and Rory was pretending to be extremely interested in the chocolate dessert ball on her plate, doing her best not to laugh.

I glanced back and forth between Jordan and Mrs. Brody, bracing myself for what came next.

My eyes went wide as a white cloud appeared over his head and began snowing little flakes of snow onto his head and shoulders. The snow began to pile up in his hair, but he didn't even seem to notice.

Jordan then sprouted antlers, and I could no longer contain myself.

My coffee dribbled from my lips, and I frantically wiped it away with my sleeve as I collapsed back in my chair in a fit of giggles.

Jordan looked so confused, which made the whole thing even funnier.

Before long, everyone at the table was laughing hysterically.

"You guys are nuts," Jordan said. "What's going on?"

I wiped tears from my eyes and tried to collect myself enough to speak, but I couldn't bring myself to talk. I was laughing too hard. I simply pointed at the mirror on the other side of the kitchen.

Jordan looked puzzled, but pushed his chair away from the table and cautiously approached the mirror.

His face paled as he looked at himself in the mirror. "What the... What did you guys do?" He joined in laughing with the rest of us and raised his hands to feel the small antlers protruding from his head.

He then turned back to us with a worried expression on his face. He pointed to his antlers. "These aren't permanent, right?"

The laughter in the room increased two-fold, and I nearly fell out of my chair.

"I can't even look at you right now," I laughed, shaking my head back and forth in sheer disbelief. "You look like Christmas threw up all over you."

"I think it suits me." He turned back towards the mirror. He then shouted and jumped about a foot in the air.

His reaction made me jump, and my heart began to beat faster in my chest. "What? What happened?"

I ran over to him and looked in the mirror. His reflection had a mind of its own and was waving back at us, smiling. I sighed and relaxed. I guessed I was still on edge from the events of the night before.

That reminded me. "Did Brett ever get back to you?"

Jordan shook his head. "No, haven't heard yet. I sent him a text and left a voice mail, so hopefully he got those."

I jumped again as a knock came from the door. A tall, dark figure stood on the other side of the window, and I stepped back cautiously as I turned towards Mrs. Brody.

"Are you expecting anyone?" I asked.

Mrs. Brody shook her head and narrowed her eyes at the door.

Jordan held his arm out, motioning for us to stay back. "I've got it."

My heart began to beat faster again as I watched

Jordan approach the door. We were still technically targets, and until we figured out who was after the ex-cops and their partners, we really weren't safe. I had let the Christmas festivities calm me a bit, but that didn't change the fact that we were in the middle of a very serious investigation.

I held my breath as Jordan opened the door.

"Oh, hey man," Jordan said as he stepped back from the open doorway. "Come in."

"Uh," Brett stared at Jordan's hair with a confused expression on his face.

"Shit," I heard Bailey whisper. Jordan's appearance suddenly went back to normal at the wave of her hand.

Brett's expression grew even more confused. "What…"

Jordan pushed the door open wider, and having noticed his appearance had changed back, he tried to act as normal as possible.

"Come in," he repeated, pretending nothing had happened.

Brett, Jordan's dark-haired friend, stepped inside. He looked at Jordan like he had just seen a ghost. I chuckled quietly to myself at that analogy. If only he knew.

"What's wrong?" Jordan asked.

Brett shook his head. "Your… Nothing. Never mind." He shook his head and turned towards the room with a smile. I snickered to myself, trying to imagine how a non-magical person would try and explain to their friend that they thought they had seen reindeer horns protruding from their head without sounding absolutely mental.

I eyed Brett as he came in and crossed my arms. He certainly wasn't my favorite person on the planet, that was for sure. The way he spoke to me when we first met made me want nothing to do with him, to be honest.

"Everyone, this is my friend Brett."

I nodded curtly, but everyone else in the room greeted him with a warm hello.

Brett smiled widely at everyone and waved. Bailey even got up and shook his hand, and I noticed a light blush creep up on her cheeks.

Oh great, just what we needed. Another asshole to break Bailey's heart.

"Come, join us," Bailey said. "Just in time for breakfast."

"Oh, thanks," Brett followed Bailey to the table and sat in the chair she pulled up for him.

Mrs. Brody got up to get him a plate and placed it in front of him on the table and began piling food onto it for him. He looked startled at first, but then let her finish her task. He didn't look like the kind of guy who was used to being mothered.

"I got your message," he finally said to Jordan after everyone settled into breakfast again. "My phone died just as I finished listening to your voicemail. I turned around and headed straight here."

"Thanks, man," Jordan said through a mouthful of pancake. "I appreciate it."

"Sounded important," Brett said. "Anything I can help with?"

I shook my head. "No, thanks. We've got it under control."

Jordan gave me a stern look, but I ignored him. All I could think of was the time we had met in October when he was a complete jerk. I realized people could have bad days, but I really didn't like this guy.

"You can go home after you eat," I said.

"Nonsense," Bailey said, smiling at him. "You've come all this way. You'll stay for a while and enjoy Christmas with us."

He smiled back at her. "Sounds great to me."

I rolled my eyes.

"Do you have the address?" I finally asked him. The least he could do was be helpful

"The what?" he said, looking confused.

"My bag," Jordan clarified. "Did you bring it?"

Brett nodded. "Yeah, right here." He reached into his own bag and brought out a smaller leather one and tossed it to Jordan.

I glowered at him but resumed eating my food. I was grateful that he at least came back to bring

Jordan his bag. He must have been driving for hours, so I guessed I couldn't be too mad.

I sighed and took another bite of sausage.

"Thanks," I finally said to Brett. "For coming back."

Jordan grinned at me but remained silent when I glared up at him. He knew that look. It was my 'I dare you to say anything' look. Points for him for being able to read me.

Jordan handed me the bag when I reached out to him, and I rummaged through it to look for the piece of paper with the address on it. When I found it, I whipped out my phone and called Sheriff Reese. I left a message when I reached his voicemail.

Bailey offered Brett the plate of chocolate balls, and when I put my phone away, I looked up to see him looking back at Bailey with a brilliant smile. He looked amused as he accepted a few chocolate balls from the tray.

I then blinked as I noticed his hair had turned a bright snow white, with silver and gold tips, and Mrs. Brody was snickering mischievously in her seat.

I couldn't help but laugh. It was certainly turning out to be an interesting Christmas.

CHAPTER ELEVEN

Finally, after about half an hour, Sheriff Reese called me back, and while the rest of the group finished breakfast, I stole away into the next room to talk.

He kept telling me to stay in the house all day while he and his men went to investigate the address.

I, obviously, wasn't going to have any of that.

"You absolutely cannot come," he lectured me through my phone. "You will stay home with Jordan and your friends and Mrs. Brody, and I'll report back if we learn anything. It doesn't make any sense for you and Jordan to come when you two are possibly the next targets."

I did my best to argue with him, but he was used to putting up with me when I tried forcing my way onto his cases. He eventually hung up on me.

"He won't let us go with him," I grumbled when I came back to the kitchen table.

"Of course, not," Jordan said. "It's too dangerous. We have to stay here until we know more."

"What?" I asked. "What do you mean, we have to stay here? You are a cop - don't you want to go investigate?"

"A retired cop," he corrected me. "Which is what got us into this mess, to begin with, remember? We're staying."

I shook my head. "No, sorry. I have to go and find out what's going on."

Jordan narrowed his eyes at me. "No. You're staying."

I rolled my eyes. He apparently didn't know how persistent I could be. I was going to go investigate, and that was that.

"You are being completely unreasonable right now," he said.

"Whatever!" I got up and left through the door towards the stairs to get my stuff. He may not want to go, but I sure as hell was going to go get to the bottom of this. I didn't trust Sheriff Reese and his goons to figure this out on their own. I grabbed my coat and bag and stormed back downstairs.

When I got back, Jordan and Brett were gone.

"Oh, what the hell?" I could hear Jordan's car as he pulled out of the driveway.

I stared after the car out the window and then turned back to the table. Everyone in the room looked just as confused as I was.

"Where'd they go?"

"Uh," Bailey began, but then shut her mouth and shrugged.

I crossed my arms and tapped my foot on the ground. "Well?"

"They went to the gala," Rory finally said.

"What?" I rubbed my eyes. "That's absolutely infuriating. I thought Jordan didn't want to go?"

"He didn't," Bailey said. "But then…"

Again, she remained quiet.

"Oh, for Pete's sake, Bailey," I said.

"Who's Pete?" she asked.

I groaned and glared at the girl. "Just come out with it!"

"Jordan got the invitation out of his bag, and suddenly he really wanted to go."

I raised my eyebrow. "That's strange."

Bailey paused. "Actually, it really was. Something didn't seem right."

Jane blinked. "You don't think it could have been spelled, do you?"

Mrs. Brody rubbed her chin thoughtfully. "You know, his sudden change in attitude did seem odd."

I looked back and forth between Jane and Mrs. Brody. "Are you two serious? Did you sense any magic in the room?"

Mrs. Brody shrugged. "No. But then again, I am getting old. The senses aren't what they used to be."

I rolled my eyes. I knew for a fact that that wasn't true. If anything, Mrs. Brody was sharper than all of us four combined.

"Come to think of it," Bailey said. "I did feel kind of strange when Brett came in, but I thought…"

Bailey began to blush.

"You have got to be kidding me!" I exclaimed. Bailey really needed to stop falling for guys at the least opportune of moments.

"Butterflies in your stomach?" I asked.

Bailey shrugged. "Maybe."

"Possibly not because a cute guy came into the room?"

She looked down at her feet. "Possibly."

I groaned. "Great! I have a bewitched boyfriend on the way to a murder site, and you lot were sitting here being giddy over a couple of boys."

Rory chewed her lip. "Well, yeah."

"Pretty much," Jane said.

"Okay," I said slowly through a deep and calming breath. For all the good it did me. I was panicking more than ever now. "This isn't good. This isn't good at all."

"What are you going to do?" Bailey asked.

"I need to go find him."

"How?" Jane asked.

"I could take Brett's car?" I suggested.

"With what keys?" Rory asked.

Dammit, good point.

"You can take me," I finally said to Rory.

She raised her eyebrows. "No way, I'm not going to meet any more murderers with you. I've had my fill, thank you very much."

I rolled my eyes. She was being melodramatic, but I guessed I couldn't force her to take me to a potentially life-threatening murder gala.

"River, it's too dangerous," Jane said. "Just call the sheriff and warn him. He'll take care of it."

I shook my head. "No. No way. Jordan's life is in danger, and I need to go make sure he's okay. Especially if the invitation was spelled! Sheriff Reese won't have a clue how to deal with that."

Bailey jumped up out of her seat. "You're right. I'll go with you."

I raised my eyebrow at her. "Oh?"

She blushed again. "Yeah, of course. To help Jordan."

I rolled my eyes. "Sure. For Jordan. Thanks, Bailey!"

I smiled at her. I was grateful for the help, and if anyone knew how to deal with a bewitching spell, it was her.

"Can we take your car?" I asked Rory.

She rolled her eyes. "Fine. Just don't get blood on the seats when you both get yourselves murdered."

"Yeah, yeah," I said. "Keys?"

Rory dug through her purse and tossed the keys at me.

"You girls be careful," Mrs. Brody said. "Turn right around if you even have the slightest inkling that something might be wrong. Promise me that."

I nodded. "Promise. We're just going to go and grab Jordan and bring him back. We'll let the police handle the rest."

Mrs. Brody eyed me and did not look convinced. Oh well, her problem. Not mine.

I pulled my jacket on and ran out the door, Bailey following closely behind.

"Take this," Mrs. Brody called from behind the door. She tossed a small bag out to Bailey, who caught it and shoved it into her purse.

"What was that?" I asked breathlessly. Man, the house sure did have a long driveway. Why the hell did Rory always insist on parking so far away from the house?

Bailey shrugged. "No idea. Something useful, I'd image. Either that or cookies. It seems really heavy, though."

I nodded. "Okay, whatever. Fine. Let's go!"

"I'll drive," she called to me as we ran down the driveway.

I tossed her the keys, and we both got in the car. In less than a few seconds we were on the road.

"Wait," I shouted suddenly.

Bailey slammed on the breaks, and the car screeched to a halt.

"What? What happened?" She looked frantic.

"We don't know where we're going, and Jordan never charged his phone so I can't call him."

"Oh, right." Bailey scrunched her face in concentration. "Didn't you call the sheriff? He'll have the address."

I nodded. "Oh, yeah. Right."

I dialed the sheriff's number, but it went straight to his voicemail. "Dammit. Voicemail."

"Do you not remember the address? You literally called him ten minutes ago."

I sighed and rubbed my eyes. "No, not really. It was at an old mill in Rockland, though. That much I remember."

"An old mill?" Bailey considered for a moment. "How many old mills can there be? I'm sure we can find it."

I shrugged. "We will have to try. Rockland is about an hour away. I'll keep calling the sheriff on the way."

Bailey sped down the winding Maine roads south along the coast towards Rockland. Luckily, it was highway most of the way, so the drive wasn't too bad. The snow had stopped, and the roads were clear, at least.

I dialed the sheriff at least half a dozen times but was met every time by his voicemail message.

I even called Jordan a few times, but I knew full well that his phone was dead.

Panic was beginning to set in as we got closer to Rockland.

It became apparent that we weren't going to get through to anybody, so I tried searching for a Rockland mill on Google on my phone.

Luckily, the first hit was exactly what we needed. An old heritage mill converted into an event space. The website looked like it hadn't been updated in ages, though.

"Bingo," I said as I put the address into the GPS system that Rory had installed in her car. "Still fifteen minutes away. Step on it!"

Rory sped down the highway as fast as she was comfortable with, which, as I couldn't help but notice through my constant nervous checking of the speedometer, was only three miles per hour over the speed limit. I was growing antsy and really didn't have another fifteen minutes of stress in me.

I distracted myself by continuing to call the sheriff and Jordan, but of course, the calls continued to meet their voicemail.

Finally, we neared the site and passed a sign with a picture of an old mill on it.

"This looks like the place," Bailey said.

She slowed the car down and turned right into a dirt road that the sign was pointing towards. The road was long and narrow and took us through a thick set of trees.

I glanced nervously at the time. It was just passed 1 pm, and I relaxed a bit. The part of the invitation that we found at Jordan's house had said the event started at 5:30 pm, so we still had quite a few hours before anything was likely to happen.

We continued to drive down the winding road, and our visibility became obscured as it began to snow. I turned and looked through the rear windshield behind us, and I could barely see anything outside through the thick trees and the snow.

"Strange place for an event," Bailey commented as I assessed our surroundings.

After another few minutes, the trees began to clear, and we could see an old wooden building far up ahead. I could barely make it out, but I thought I saw cars up ahead as well.

"I think that's the sheriff's car." I pointed to way to the right-hand side of the mill, a bit farther down along the road.

"Looks like it," Bailey said. "Let's go see."

Bailey drove us around the mill towards the other cars, which had parked a fair distance away from the building behind a thick cluster of trees.

"Why did they park so far away?" Bailey asked.

I shrugged. "Probably to remain hidden behind the trees. Better park here, too."

Bailey pulled the car up beside the sheriff's, and I noticed a little ways away was Jordan's car, as well.

"We're definitely in the right spot," I said. I squinted through the snow around the car, but couldn't see anyone else.

"I wonder where they all went?" Bailey asked. "I don't see them around the cars."

I shrugged. "Who knows. But we had better go try and find them before anything bad happens. I have a bad feeling about this."

Bailey nodded. "Alright. Let's go inside."

CHAPTER TWELVE

Bailey and I walked up to the mill in silence. I had my hand on my phone in case we needed to call for help, although given the failed attempts in the past hours, I had a feeling it was a false confidence.

Bailey held her purse up as if it was a weapon, ready to strike.

It was absolutely silent apart from the crunching of snow beneath our footsteps.

"It doesn't really look like there's an event going on here," Bailey whispered as we approached the structure.

I shook my head. "It doesn't actually even look like there's been any events here in a long time."

As we got closer towards the mill, I noticed it looked like it hadn't been maintained in years. The wood siding had fallen off in a few places, and some of the windows were broken.

Bailey shrugged. "Maybe they think it's rustic charm?"

I didn't think so.

I searched the ground for footprints to see where everyone else had gone, but the snow covered any evidence of other people. For all we knew, they could have been captured and taken somewhere else.

Bailey and I walked around to the front of the building, which was facing away from where we had parked. I walked up and put my ear against the front door to listen.

"I think somebody's inside," I said. I could hear the faint muffled sounds of conversation.

"Do you think it's them?" Bailey asked.

I sure hoped so. The alternative would be that they had already been captured and it was the murderer that I could hear inside. I swallowed hard, trying to push that thought from my mind.

"Better stay quiet, just in case," I said.

I slowly pulled the front door open and stepped inside to the small entryway. There was another set of double doors in front of us, leading to the inside of the mill.

I motioned for Bailey to follow me, and I pulled the second set of doors open. The doors creaked loudly, and Bailey and I immediately pressed our backs up against the wall to remain hidden from anyone who might have been inside. After a few moments of holding my breath and not hearing anything on the other side of the door, though, I relaxed and stepped back toward the door.

Before stepping in, I peeked my head around the door to look inside.

It was dark. The small windows of the mill were so dusty and covered in dirt that barely any light leaked inside. It took a moment for my eyes to adjust after being outside in the glaring daylight.

I couldn't see anything inside, so we both stepped through the doors and closed them behind us.

A deep shiver ran through my body, and I turned to see Bailey had felt the same thing. She looked pale and was shaking her head.

"I don't like this," she murmured. "There's something wrong. There's something not right with this place."

I nodded. "I can feel it, too."

I then noticed a small light in the far corner of the large interior space, but a moment later it was extinguished, and I could no longer see where it came from.

"Shit," I whispered. "Something is over there."

I stepped back towards the door and gave it a push, but it wouldn't budge.

I then turned back towards the door and gave the handle a squeeze and shoved the door with my shoulder, but still it wouldn't open.

"Bailey," I whispered in panic. "I think we're

locked in."

Bailey tried the door herself. "What? Why would it lock from the inside?"

We gave each other nervous looks and turned our attention back towards the indoor space. Something was going on, and I suddenly really didn't care to hang around and find out.

My heart began to beat faster as I heard a floorboard creak from the far side of the room.

"H.. Hello?" I called out in a loud whisper. "Who's there?"

Suddenly a bright light was on me, and a man stepped out of the shadows before us. "Put your hands where I can see them!" he shouted.

Bailey and I obliged, but when I saw who it was through the light in my face, I lowered my hands back down.

"Oh, man," I said. "Seriously? Did you really have to scare us like that?"

Sheriff Reese had his gun out, and Jordan's friend Brett was holding up a flashlight.

"Oh, it's you, River," the sheriff said. "What the hell are you two doing here? I told you both to stay at home."

Jordan and the other officers walked into the light as well, and Jordan did not look impressed.

I motioned towards him and raised my eyebrows at the sheriff. "You told him to stay home, too, but you don't seem too concerned about his being here."

Sheriff Reese put his gun back in its holster and crossed his arms. "Jordan O'Riley is an ex-cop. He knows how to handle himself."

I rolled my eyes. "Yeah, and is it not ex-cops who were the targets of the kidnappings, and possible murders?"

"Ex-cops, yes," Sheriff Reese repeated, "and their partners." He narrowed his eyes at me.

I shrugged. "Well, it really doesn't seem like there's anything going on here, anyway. Maybe we got the whole thing wrong?"

Sheriff Reese shrugged. "Could be, but we can't be too sure. The boys and I are going to hang around until the event is supposed to start, at least, to see if anyone shows up. Chances are, this whole thing was a ruse."

"That doesn't answer the question about why all those people went missing," Jordan commented.

"Or about why two ghosts appeared in my bedroom yesterday morning to tell me I was going to die," I added.

No, I had a feeling it definitely wasn't a ruse. "Maybe we just got the address wrong."

Bailey nodded. "I hope so. Can we leave? This place gives me the creeps."

"Me, too. I can't quite put my finger on it, but I

know I don't want to be here anymore." I held my hand up to shade my eyes from the light Brett was still shining in my face, blinding me. "Can you guys feel it?"

They all shook their heads.

"All I feel is cold and damp," Brett said. "And blind. Let's find the damn lights."

"There was a breaker in the back that I noticed," one of the officers commented. "I'll go check it out."

Brett followed with the flashlight, leaving Bailey and me in the dark with Jordan and Sheriff Reese. We glanced at each other and smirked, as his hair was still the shimmery white and silver that Mrs. Brody spelled on him. I wondered if he even knew? No one else must have said anything.

I couldn't see much through the darkness, but I could sense the anger and tension both men were carrying. Sheriff Reese took in a breath, and I had a feeling he was about to lecture us about coming here.

Before he had a chance to say anything, though, I managed to get a word in.

"Jordan, what made you change your mind and come?"

Jordan shrugged and scratched his chin. "Not sure. I just suddenly really needed to come check it out. I couldn't miss it - not if I could come help in some way. Besides, I didn't want to miss the event."

I narrowed my eyes at him. "I thought you said you didn't want to go to the event after all?"

"A man can change his mind."

"Uh-huh," I said, glancing sidelong at Bailing beside me. "Hand over the invitation."

Jordan shook his head. "No. Why?"

"Just pass it to me."

"No, it's tucked away in my pocket."

I turned toward Bailey, who had a look of extreme concern on her eyes. "Dude, you're bewitched."

"Hand me the invitation," I repeated.

"No."

I groaned. He was being exceptionally stubborn, and I really didn't have time to be playing games at that moment. I didn't care if he was bewitched, he was still being exceedingly irritating.

I lunged forward and grabbed his belt with one hand, and reached into his back pocket with another. He tried to push me off, but he was too slow.

"Got it!" I held the small torn piece of paper up to Bailey to inspect.

"Do you feel anything from it?" Bailey asked.

I shook my head. "No, am I supposed to?"

She took the invitation from me and turned it over in her hands. Sheriff Reese and Jordan were watching her curiously, but Jordan made no attempt to take the paper back. In fact, I noticed his body posture seemed to relax a bit after I took it from him. The spell must have had a serious affect on the guy.

Bailey considered the object in her hand a moment, holding it up close to her eyes to try and see better through the darkness.

"The invitation has your name on it, right?" she asked Jordan.

Jordan nodded. "Yeah."

"Did it have River's name as well?"

"No, just my name plus one."

Bailey nodded. "I suspect you're not feeling the spell because you're already a magic user. Even though your name's not on it, you are still technically his plus one. In any other situation, I would suspect the bewitchment would carry over to whoever the partner was."

I sighed. "That's so twisted. Who would spell an invitation?"

Sheriff Reese looked concerned. "Someone who really wanted the invitees to come to the event."

Oh right, that.

The indoor lights turned on just then, and we all raised our hands to prevent our eyes from being blinded. It took a solid few moments before I could open my eyes again. The light burned red through my eyelids, and I squinted through brightness around me until my eyes adjusted.

Bailey and I then gasped at once, and I stepped back and pressed my back against the door.

"What's going on?" Jordan asked, trying to follow our gaze into the middle of the room, but obviously not seeing what we saw.

I shook my head and repeated, "No, no, no..."

Bailey slid down onto her feet and buried her head in her hands and began to cry.

"What the hell is going on?" Brett asked as he joined the group.

My skin grew cold and clammy, and I wasn't even sure my heart was beating in my chest. The scene in front of me was too much to be able to process all at once.

The men in the room continued to look around but grew angry when they couldn't figure out what we were freaking out about.

"There's dozens of them," I finally whispered. My eyes were wide and dry, but I couldn't bring myself to blink.

"All of them. They're all dead."

I stared into the middle of the room, and Jordan finally walked up to me and shook me by the shoulder.

"River," he said as he looked into my eyes. My gaze blurred and I couldn't even focus on him. "What's going on? What do you see?"

I shook my head and tried to speak again, but my voice had dried up as well. I simply pointed into the middle of the room, which obviously didn't help any.

There were ghosts. There were dozens of ghosts, lingering around the interior of the mill. They all just sort of stood there, motionless, looking around themselves with blank expressions.

That explained why Bailey and I had felt weird when we came inside. The place was full of the spirits of dead people. And as I looked around the room, I recognized their faces from the missing persons articles I had studied so thoroughly the past two days.

"Can someone tell me what the hell is going on here?" Sheriff Reese demanded. "River, what's going on?"

I took a steadying breath and placed my hand on Bailey's shoulder for stability. She had stopped crying out loud, but I could feel her body shudder through silent sobs.

"Ghosts," I finally whispered. "The ghosts of the missing people. All of them. They're all here."

The sheriff and Jordan started looking frantically around the room but turned back towards me when they still couldn't see anything.

"Where?" Jordan asked.

I stared into the room. "Everywhere. So many of them."

I was grateful that the sheriff didn't question me. After the past few months, he had grown accustomed to the paranormal stuff. He didn't believe any of it at first, but after the latest local murder, I figured he had begun to catch on. It was a testament to his intelligence, and I realized I never give the guy enough credit for what he does.

Brett and the other officers, on the other hand, looked amused, and their expressions suggested that we were all crazy.

"Are you drunk?" Brett finally asked me.

I sighed, but thankfully I didn't have to explain myself.

Sheriff Reese turned towards his men and cleared his throat. His voice took on an air of authority, and his men looked to him attentively as he spoke.

"I don't care what your belief systems are," he began, "but today, you listen to everything these girls have to say. Understood? You are to believe everything that comes out of their mouths, and you are to listen to their advice."

Both officers nodded and glanced towards me with strange expressions in their eyes. They both then nodded to me, and I attempted a small smile back.

"I'll do my best not to spook you," I managed to say.

Brett, on the other hand, was having none of it. "You guys are batshit crazy, you know that?"

Jordan grabbed his friends shoulder and turned him to look straight in his eyes.

"Look, man," Jordan said. "I know you're all

iffy with the whole paranormal thing, but whether you believe it or not, it's real. I've seen it first hand, and I have a feeling tonight you will, too. So just swallow your pride, and follow along. Okay?"

Brett looked as if he was going to hit Jordan for a moment, but then his expression softened, and he nodded his agreement. "Sure, man. Anything for you."

I blew out a sigh and then took a few steps forward towards the middle of the room.

"So, what are we going to do about the ghosts?" I asked.

Sheriff Reese shrugged his shoulders. "That's your area of expertise, River. I just need you to find out what happened to them, and why they're all here."

The chill I felt earlier had left, and I was now filled with a hot determination to solve this case. Something terrible had happened to these people, and it was up to me to figure it out.

I glanced down at Bailey, who was still on the ground in a fit, and I realized I might be on my own for this.

I motioned for Jordan to go help her, and he went to join Bailey on the floor and put his arm around her.

I then pushed up my sleeves and stepped into the middle of the room to join the spirits.

They regarded me curiously, but they all

remained silent. Eerily silent. It wasn't like spirits to just hover, and I suspected that whatever had happened here had scared them into silence.

I had a feeling it was going to be a very challenging day.

CHAPTER THIRTEEN

SHERIFF REESE WAS PROVIDING ME WITH QUESTIONS to interrogate the spirits with, but it was useless. None of them would speak with me, and they all looked so frightened.

Bailey had finally gathered herself, and she came to join me in the middle of the room.

"Any progress?" she asked.

I shook my head. "No, nothing. They must have been fairly traumatized for them all to be staying so silent."

Bailey looked around the room then looked back at me and shrugged. "I don't see any sign of bodies or a struggle. Do you think they were killed here?"

I nodded thoughtfully. "Yeah, I do. Why else would they be hanging around?"

Bailey shivered. "I really don't like it in here."

"I bet they don't, either."

I tried approaching a different ghost to see if I would have any better luck. It wasn't as if they couldn't see us or anything. They all acknowledged me when I went up to them, but they all just seemed too scared to speak.

I spent what felt like a few hours trying different approaches to no avail. Sheriff Reese nearly gave up, and I wasn't going to be too far behind him.

I spent my time analyzing the room. It was a large space, mainly just one open room, with an entry in the front and a small area behind a wall in the back. The spirits were all clustered together in the main space, and they seemed to be avoiding the doors and windows.

"Did you notice they're all dressed in dresses and suits?" Bailey asked.

I looked through the crowd, back and forth between the spirits of the men and women around us. "Yeah, you're right. They must have all gotten the same invitation as Jordan."

Bailey frowned. "But for different nights?"

I shrugged. "Well, it's not like the event was actually real. I suspect he was using it as a way to lure these people here. The only question is, why?"

Bailey shivered again and held her arms tight around her stomach. "It's so sad. All these people. They all look so young. They thought they were coming to an event to celebrate. Not to die."

I nodded as I began pacing the room, trying to

read the faces of the spirits around me. "Yeah, it's pretty sick."

"Were Sarah and Peter dressed up?" Bailey asked.

"I actually can't remember." I continued to walk around, but my attempts at conversation were met with frightened stares and silence.

"Hello," I finally said to about the twentieth spirit I approached. "We're here to help you and figure out what happened here. Are you able to answer a few questions for me?"

The young woman stared back at me but kept her silence.

I sighed. "My name is River. What's yours?"

The spirit's eyes went wide at the mention of my name. That was at least some progress.

I waited patiently, hoping that she would say something. I breathed out a sigh of relief when she finally opened her mouth to speak.

"Jordan?" she whispered quietly to me.

I nodded and motioned back to the other side of the room. "Yes. He's over there."

Her eyes went even wider.

"Run," she whispered again.

My heart began to beat a little faster in my chest.

"Why?" I asked. "What's going on here? What happened to you all?"

The spirit simply looked back down to her feet and wandered away to join the rest of her group, sulking around looking defeated, devastated, and scared.

I rubbed my eyes and groaned. "We're not getting anywhere."

Bailey put her hand on my shoulder. "Well, at least we know that Sarah and Peter weren't lying. If this spirit knows your name, then it at least confirms our suspicions."

I nodded. "You're right. At least there's that."

"It also means," she began, "that we really need to get you and Jordan out of here."

I shook my head. "Not until we get to the bottom of this."

"River, we need to go," Bailey insisted. She grabbed my arm and tried to pull me away, but in her attempt to drag me through the room she tripped over a raised floorboard and fell onto the ground, spilling the contents of her purse everything.

I rolled my eyes. "And you call me clumsy."

Brett walked over to her and began helping her pick up her things. The small bag Mrs. Brody had given her had fallen out and was lying on the floor a few feet away.

I eyed the bag as I began to sense something strange coming from it, but my attention was immediately turned back to Brett as he bent over and revealed something that was under his shirt.

"Gun!" I shouted as I ran backward. "He's got a gun!"

I pointed frantically at Brett so Sheriff Reese and his men could see, but they just stood there staring at me.

"What the hell are you guys waiting for?" I screamed. "He has a gun! Why the hell does he have a gun?"

I knew there was something off with that guy since the moment I met him with Ryan Bramley around Halloween. Of course, it made sense that he had something to do with this. Ryan ended up being a murderer, after all. Why not him, too?

"Do something!" I was beginning to panic. "Bailey, run!"

Bailey had began crawling backward away from her, her eyes wide and her face pale.

But Jordan simply walked up to him in the middle of the room and crossed his arms as he gave me a strange look.

"River, he's a cop," Jordan said to me.

"He's a what?"

"A cop. That's how we know each other. We used to work together."

I blinked and stared back and forth between the two men.

"What did you think?" Jordan asked. "Did you actually think he was here to hurt us?"

I shrugged. "I don't know. It makes sense. We were meant to be lured here, to begin with. It was just as easy for him to bring you here on his own. We're both here, aren't we?"

Jordan shook his head. "River, he's okay. He's one of the good guys."

I glowered. From his crappy attitude towards me when we first met, I severely doubted that. Not that I held a grudge, or anything.

When Jordan continued to look at me with an expression of mild anger and exasperation, I sighed and gave in. "Okay, fine. Sorry, Brett."

Brett nodded at me and pulled his shirt back down to cover his gun.

I relaxed somewhat and turned my attention back to the bag on the floor.

"Bailey, what did Mrs. Brody give you?" There was something strange emanating from the bag, and it had a strangely familiar feeling to it.

Bailey shrugged and walked over to it to inspect the contents of the pouch. She gasped as she looked inside, and reached in to slam the little box shut.

She then lifted the box to show me, and I couldn't help but laugh.

"What did she have in mind for us to do with that?" I asked.

Bailey shrugged. "I don't know, but I'm sure she had a very good reason."

The spirits that were standing around near the box began to look happier, suddenly.

I blinked and was confused for a moment, but

then realized what was happening. "Of course," I said. "The holiday spirit. That woman is a genius."

Bailey caught on and smiled back at me. "Oh. Clever!"

Mrs. Brody had obviously figured we would need some sort of a pick-me-up, and that might just have been the thing to pull these spirits out of their funk.

"Open it again," I said. "But just a little bit. We don't know the full effects of that stuff."

Jordan approached us in the middle of the room and looked inquisitively at the small box. "What's in there?"

"Might want to step back," I laughed.

He did so instantly, having learned to trust me with these sorts of things. He was all too familiar with the strange knickknacks we had lying around the house, having experienced first-hand the strange and wonderful things Mrs. Brody liked to leave out for unsuspecting visitors.

Bailey opened the box for a moment and waved it around the air in front of her. She then closed it tightly and shoved it back into the bag for safe keeping.

The spirits around her gained a new life, so to speak. One even began humming a Christmas tune.

"Hello," I said to a middle-aged man who stood next to Bailey. "What's your name?"

The man smiled at me, his eyes sparkling with

the magic of Christmas spirit. "I'm Jon. Pleased to meet you, ma'am."

I smiled back at him. "Nice to meet you, Jon. Mind if we ask you a few questions?"

With their newfound happy dispositions, due to the holiday spirit Bailey released into the environment, our interrogation began to go much smoothly. Sheriff Reese joined us in the middle of the room, and while he didn't understand what possibly could have changed, he offered his help in providing the right questions to ask. I repeated their answers for those in the room who wouldn't see or hear them.

"Why does it suddenly feel festive in here?" Brett asked.

I shrugged. "No idea. I think you're imagining things.

"No, I swear," he said. "I can hear jingle bells."

"I can smell gingerbread," Jordan said.

I laughed. "You guys are crazy." Bailey and I eyed each other and burst into a fit of giggles.

The two other officers were avoiding us, clearly not wanting anything to do with the strange witchcraft that was obviously going on in the center of the room. They circled the outer edges of the mill, keeping an eye out for us. It was too bad, really, as if anyone in this room needed holiday spirit, it was those two.

Jordan shook his head in amazement. "I have no idea what's going on, but it's amazing."

Brett just looked confused but kept his mouth shut. He recognized the benefits of whatever was going on and left us in peace to continue our investigation.

We spoke with the spirits for another hour or so before the effects of the magic wore off, and by that time it had already gotten dark out. Not that the windows let much light through in the first place, but that muted glow that came in through the dusty panes of glass had finally disappeared. I guessed it was around five o'clock, and confirmed it by checking my phone.

"Hey," I said to Jordan as realization dawned on me. "Isn't it about time for the gala?"

He nodded. "Yeah, it should be happening pretty soon. Doesn't look like much is going on, though."

I looked around the dusty old mill, and it was evident that there would be no event happening there.

I then froze and strained my ears when I thought I heard a noise off in the distance.

"Do you guys hear that?" I asked.

Everyone else began looking around, and Sheriff Reese held his hand in the air motioning for everyone to be quiet.

There is was - faint, and barely audible - the sound of a car coming.

"Quick, turn out the lights," I whispered frantically.

Brett ran to switch the light off at the back of the room, and we all gathered together behind the wall near the back of the mill.

We stood huddled together in silence, listening for any clue as to who might be coming.

I heard two clicks and Brett as the sheriff brought out their guns and held them at the ready.

I held my breath, waiting, as the sound of the vehicle came closer towards us.

CHAPTER FOURTEEN

I CLUTCHED JORDAN'S ARM AS WE ALL HID BEHIND the back wall of the mill. We all held our breath as the sound of a vehicle came up and stopped right next to the far wall. The windows were illuminated by the headlights for a moment, and then we were met with blackness again.

I could hear the faint sound of footsteps in snow and then the creak of the front door.

I tried to peer through a slit in the wooden wall, but my visibility was minimal.

Sheriff Reese was up on his tiptoes looking through a crack in the wall, which looked larger and easier to see through than mine did.

Exterior lights were turned on outside the front door.

I squinted and tried to see as best I could. I could

make out a tall, thin form silhouetted in front of the light.

"Who is that?" Bailey whispered.

I nudged her with my elbow to be quiet. We couldn't risk being heard until we knew who the person was or what was going on.

The instant the person stepped into the room – he looked like a male - the entire space lit up with commotion. The ghosts began chattering frantically amongst themselves at the arrival of whoever it was.

I grabbed Bailey's arm and squeezed hard. The energy in the room dramatically changed, and I got chills all over my body. The hairs on my arms stood on end, and I really didn't like the feeling of it.

Something bad was going on, and I desperately needed to know what.

The person slowly walked into the room, and I say he was carrying a large bag with him.

The spirits were catatonic, murmuring worriedly amongst themselves and shouting things at the man. There were at least thirty voices all chattering at once, and I couldn't make out anything they were saying.

It was completely disorienting, and Bailey was holding her hands over her ears to block out the noise.

A moment later, the person dropped the bag on the ground and shouted in a low male voice, "SHUT UP!"

I jumped and nearly fell backward onto the floor. Bailey did the same, only she did actually stumble onto the floor. Fortunately, the noise from the spirits in the next room muffled her fall.

I clasped my hands over my mouth and did my best not to scream.

Jordan, Brett, Sheriff Reese and the officers were staring at us with wide eyes; anger and worry spread across their faces.

"What the hell?" the sheriff mouthed to me.

I stared up at him with wide eyes, my breath caught in my throat.

"He's a witch," I whispered to him, pointing through the walls. "He can hear the ghosts."

That made things just that little bit more complicated. It was a good thing Bailey and I had shown up. For the men's' sake, definitely not for ours. It could end very, very badly if we weren't careful.

I helped Bailey back up onto her feet and peered through the hole in the wall again to watch.

"Why don't they just go in and arrest him?" Bailey whispered to me.

Working with the sheriff so much these past few months, I had gained a lot of insight into how these types of things worked. Not only that, but I wrote about this stuff all the time in the paper back at school, whenever a bust went down in Manhattan. It happened all too frequently, which was scary, but it made for great article content.

"Because he hasn't done anything wrong," I whispered back. "If we go out now, we'll spook him away, and we might lose the opportunity to catch him. If we wait for him to do something then the sheriff can arrest him, and he can be put away for good."

Bailey nodded silently. "What do you think he's going to do?"

I shook my head. "I don't know, but by the reaction the ghosts gave, I doubt it's anything good."

I heard the faint crumpling of paper from beside me and glanced down to see Jordan fidgeting with the invitation in his hand.

"How the hell did you get that back?" I whispered angrily to him. It had been in my pocket. The sneaky bastard must have slipped it out when I wasn't paying attention.

I tried to reach for it, but he pulled it away quickly and glared down at me. Looking into his ice blue eyes, I could barely recognize him. I guessed we had been right, the invitation had bewitched him.

I pulled my hand away slowly so as to not make him react, and made a point of keeping an eye on him in case he did anything stupid. I had no idea what the spell was intended for, but I suspected it had something to do with the mill and that guy. Jordan fidgeted with it nervously, and his eyes were darting back and forth as it he was trying to decide something complicated.

"Jordan," I whispered to him.

He raised his eyebrow at me.

"The invitation is spelled," I said. "It's bewitched you. Let me have the paper, please."

He glared at me again and placed the invitation in his pocket.

I sighed. So much for appealing to his reasonable side.

I waved my arm to get the sheriff's attention, and when he finally looked at me, I motioned from my eyes then towards Jordan, signaling for him to keep an eye on him.

He nodded his understanding and turned back towards the hole in the wall, the whole while keeping his hand on his gun at his side.

The floorboards creaked as the man began walking towards us. I held my breath and willed my heart to stop beating so loudly. I felt as if everyone in the room could hear the thumping in my chest, and I tried to breathe deeply to try and slow my heart rate.

The amount of stress I was in seemed unreasonable, though, as we were seven and he was one. But given the situation, what with dozens of spirits on the other side of the wall that were likely victims of the person in the next room, I had my suspicions that he was capable of some pretty serious stuff.

The man walked towards our wall in the dark but flicked the light on just before he reached us and turned around to face the center of the room again.

I let out a breath I had been holding and tried to rack my brain to see if I could remember any spells that might help us in this situation. Unfortunately, I had never had the need to learn anything too defensive, and I was coming up dry.

I could see easier through the wall now that the man had turned the interior lights on. It was strange, hiding like we were. Watching. I felt like I was in some sort of spy novel or James Bond movie.

The man walked back toward the center of the room and opened his bag. He then began removing objects and laying them on the floor around him.

When he finally turned around to face the back of the room, I realized it was no man at all, but a teenage boy. He couldn't have been more than seventeen years old.

"What's he doing?" Bailey whispered.

"No idea, but I don't think it's good," I replied.

The spirits in the room had retreated from the boy and were all hovering nervously around the perimeter of the room. They had grown silent again, and the air was thick with their fear. I could feel it in my bones, that's how strong the energy in the air was.

"I need to go to him," Jordan said suddenly as he moved back from the wall and stepped towards the edge.

Brett reached out and grabbed his shoulder and pulled him back.

"Don't you bloody dare," he whispered. "You're staying right here until we know more about this kid."

Jordan yanked his shoulder free and tried to walk again to the edge of the wall, but Sheriff Reese and his officers were on him as well, restraining him by his arms.

"You stay right where you are," the sheriff insisted.

Jordan struggled against their restraint, but couldn't pull himself free. He looked angry and determined and fought hard to get out of their grip.

Their struggle wasn't exactly quiet, and I anxiously looked back from the hole in the wall to the situation occurring behind me. The boy in the main room didn't seem to be able to hear anything, but I doubted that would last if Jordan decided to make any more noise.

"Get the paper," Bailey urged.

I tried to approach Jordan, but he kicked me away.

"Jerk," I muttered as I rubbed the area on my thigh where he had made impact.

I attempted to reach for his pocket again, but he jerked away from me.

He then twisted to try and get out of the grip he was in, but he fell down onto his back with a loud thud during the attempt, and the rest of the guys fell on and around him.

I gasped as they made impact, and quickly turned to look back through the hole in the wall toward the teenager in the next room.

I could feel my skin grow cold when I realized he had heard, and pulled away from the opening in the wall when I saw his dark, narrow eyes staring right back at me.

I held my hand over my chest and tried to calm my breathing while telling myself there was no way he could have seen me through that tiny hole.

None the less, I was terrified and had to come up with a plan, and fast.

I peered back through the hole and saw that the kid was walking towards us with something long and sharp in his hands.

Just when he got close enough to the wall to nearly see us, though, one of the spirits in the far side of the room shouted something at him.

I couldn't make out what he had said, but it was enough to draw the kid's attention back away from us.

I stood frozen, listening to his footsteps grow quieter as he walked away from our wall.

"That was close," I whispered. I nearly giggled, I was so relieved.

I supposed the sheriff or Brett or one of the officers could have shot him if he had done anything, but somehow that didn't bring any comfort to my thoughts.

I glanced down at the men on the floor and extended a hand to offer to help them up. Then, sneakily, as Jordan was pushing himself off the ground, I reached into his pocket and pulled out the invitation.

He nearly punched me as a result, but I was lucky that Brett was standing right next to him, and he grabbed Jordan's wrist before he had a chance to extend it toward me.

"Thank you," I whispered to him.

Brett nodded. "Don't mention it."

Jordan stared at me angrily, but then after a moment his expression began to soften. He then shook his head and ran his hands over his face, and when he looked down at me with those big ice blue eyes, I could tell that he was back to his normal self.

"Oh god, River," he whispered, stepping towards me. "I'm so sorry. I don't know what got into me."

I waved the invitation in the air in front of me, ensuring I was standing outside of his reach. "I do. The invitation has bewitched you. Better leave this with me."

Jordan blinked and stared down at the piece of

paper. "How can such a small thing have so much power?"

I laughed quietly. "Oh, you'd be surprised."

Jordan nodded. "I'm so sorry. I just... I just really needed to go see that guy in the other room. I felt such a strong urge to go approach him."

"Well," I said. "I guess that confirms who spelled the invitation." I glanced over to Sheriff Reese, who nodded back at me. I was grateful that he was following along. I made a mental note never to underestimate that guy again.

My attention turned back toward the wall as the ghosts began making a commotion again.

"What's happening?" Jordan whispered.

I squinted through the hole and noticed the ghosts rushing around the room, murmuring amongst themselves. I couldn't quite make out what they were saying too clearly, but I thought I heard one of them repeating "another one, another one."

"Silence," the boy whispered loudly to the room around him. "Do you want to ever be allowed out of here, or not?"

The spirits immediately went silent again.

Ah, so that's why none of them had left. I wondered if he had cast a spell capturing them all inside? I also wondered how Sarah and Peter managed to escape to come warn me about the danger I was in.

Come to think of it, I wonder why they hadn't

remembered Jordan's name, given the fact that he was the ex-cop of the relationship. So many questions, I would have to make a point of getting answers after this ordeal was over.

If we survived it, that was.

The boy pulled a black jacket from the bag on the floor and put it on. He then picked up a tray and placed some small objects on it. From where I stood, it looked like some sort of decanter and two glasses. He then walked towards the front door carrying the tray like a waiter and stood near the closed doors.

"What's he doing?" I whispered.

The boy stood by the front door and waited, completely still, for quite a few minutes.

The chatter from the spirits began picking up again, but this time more quietly.

I wanted to go and ask one of them what was going on, but I didn't want to risk being seen or heard. Unfortunately, none of the ghosts were near enough to our hiding spot to ask them anything.

Finally, after about twenty minutes, I heard a car pull up near the mill outside.

I gasped and turned to look at Sheriff Reese.

He stared back at me with wide eyes, his hand twitching over his gun.

"Someone's here," I whispered.

We all turned towards the far side wall of the mill, but the windows were too clouded, and we couldn't see much through the glass.

I heard two car doors slam shut, and the quiet sound of footsteps through the snow.

A moment later, the front doors creaked open, and then a knock sounded against the inner doors leading to the inside of the mill.

I peered through the hole in the wall unblinkingly, desperate to catch every last movement that I could.

Soft voices echoed in through the room, and the boy led the newcomers into the main space, the front doors shutting behind them.

The spirits had pressed themselves up against the side wall. Many of them, I noticed, were looking the other way or covering their eyes with their hands. Whatever was about to happen, they didn't want to watch.

As the boy and the couple neared the center of the room and removed their coats, I noticed the two newcomers were a young-looking couple dressed in a tuxedo and a long, formal dress.

I inhaled a sharp breath. "Oh shit."

CHAPTER FIFTEEN

"Wow," the woman said. "This place is amazing."

"Yeah, it's pretty neat," her partner agreed, "but it doesn't look like there's anything going on here. Did we get the right address?"

The teenager nodded to them and held out his tray. "Indeed, you have come to the right address. Unfortunately, there has been a last-minute change in venue."

"Oh," the man looked confused.

"Just wait here, and a limousine will come take you to the correct venue. I was instructed to stay here and inform our guests of the change. Why don't you have a drink while we wait?"

The man nodded. "Okay, sure. Thank you."

"You must be River and Jordan," the boy said, as

he adjusted his tray in his hand so he could pour the drinks.

I gasped suddenly and clamped my hand over my mouth. I then glanced over to Jordan, who looked back at me with worried eyes.

"No, Jules," the man said. "And this is Bernie."

I turned my attention back towards the main room.

"Ah," the boy said, setting the decanter down on the tray without pouring anything. "You're early. Quite early."

It could have just been me, but I thought the boy's voice suddenly sounded a bit nervous. He began fidgeting awkwardly with his left hand and stepped nervously back and forth between both feet. He craned his head sideways to look out the window but seemed content with what he saw. Or what he didn't see, I supposed. I had a feeling he was looking for Jordan and me, as it was now just past the time our invitation told us to arrive.

"We weren't sure how the roads were going to be, so we gave ourselves some extra time," the man named Jules said.

"And good thing we did," Bernie added. "We might have missed the limousine!"

The teenager nodded and regained his composure somewhat. He finally filled the glasses from the decanter and offered them to the couple, who accepted them graciously.

"Was the event actually supposed to be here?" the woman asked. "It's so... old."

The teenager laughed. "I suppose they were going for old country charm. Fortunately, they found a much better venue. I assure you, the wait will be worth it."

I watched the interaction anxiously through the wall and wanted desperately to go in and intervene.

Unfortunately, I knew that would ruin any chance we had of figuring out what was going on, and Sheriff Reese would never forgive me.

It wasn't easy sitting back and watching, though. It felt as if a bomb was about to go off, and there was nothing I could do but watch the clock count down.

I glanced back at the group, who all stood up against the wall quietly. Sheriff Reese and Jordan were looking through gaps in the wall, and the rest had their ears up against the rough wood, listening intently to what was going on on the other side.

"I'm going to go wait in the car," the woman said. "It's cold in here."

I watched her walk towards the door and push on the handle, but nothing budged.

She turned back towards the teenager. "The door is locked."

"That's funny," the boy said. "It shouldn't be."

The woman tried pushing the door again with

one hand, but she couldn't get it to open. "No, it's locked."

I turned to look at Bailey, who had gone ghostly pale again.

I never understood that term, actually, as ghosts weren't actually pale. Not that it was the time to consider such things, though, given the circumstances.

"What do we do?" Bailey whispered.

I turned to look at the sheriff, who held his hand out signaling for me to stay put. I could tell he recognized the expression on my face. He raised both hands together in a pleading gesture, and I sighed and nodded my understanding. I would just have to sit still and let him manage the situation. He was the sheriff, after all.

"We have to wait until we have reason enough to stop him," the sheriff whispered.

I nodded. "I know, I know. But what exactly are we looking for? We have no idea what he's going to do."

"Keep an eye out for any sort of weapon," he replied.

I shook my head and peered back through the wall. "I don't think he's going to use a weapon."

I waited and watched as the three people in the next room conversed. The woman, Bernie, was standing near the door, and the two men were chatting between themselves in a friendly manner. Everything seemed normal enough.

I looked sideways towards one of the nearest ghosts. I didn't see any wounds or anything suggesting they were brutally attacked in life. There was absolutely no sign of struggle at all, in fact. I looked around at the other ghosts around and noticed the same on them, too. They all simply looked like they dressed up in their finest outfits and stepped away from their human bodies.

"Sheriff," I whispered. "He's not going to use a weapon. None of the ghosts show any signs of being attacked."

The sheriff looked toward me and considered a moment. "Okay, then what? What do we look for?"

I shook my head. "I don't know."

I continued to watch through the wall, hoping the teenager would show some sort of sign of pre-emptive attack so we could run out and stop him before he hurt anyone. I bet he didn't have a team of cops, ex-cops, and witches in the building during the last time he did this, so maybe we would get lucky.

"Here, let me try the door," the boy said. "Sometimes these old buildings do that. I'm sure it's just the rust."

Bernie stepped away from the door and took her partner's hand as the boy approached the door.

"So, Jules," the boy said as he fidgeted with the front door handle. "Congratulations on your retirement. What made you decide to leave the force?" The kid's voice took on a bitter tone as he asked the question, but Jules didn't seem to notice.

"Had a bad case with a lost kid," Jules replied. "It was just too much for me, I couldn't take on another case like it. Being a cop just wasn't for me, I guess."

"So, you abandoned your job?" the boy asked.

My breathing quickened as I listened to them speak.

"Get out," I whispered. "Get out, now. Can't you tell he's angry at you?" I wanted to shout through the wall for Jules and Bernie to run, but I did my best to hold my tongue. The moment the sheriff gave the okay, I would be ready, though. The kid obviously had some serious anger towards cops. Or ex-cops, rather.

"You can put it that way, I guess," Jules sounded defeated, as if he had been carrying the guilt of leaving with him for a while.

Bernie wrapped her arm around him and squeezed. "You didn't abandon it. You put in your time and your energy, and now it's time for you to move on."

"Tell me about this kid," the boy said.

Jules sighed and took a long sip of his drink. "I haven't talked about it in a while, actually. There was a young kid who lived down the street from my parents. He had gone missing, and me and the boys spent a week out searching for him."

"What happened?"

"We found him ten days later, in the woods, naked and missing his right arm. He was about the same age as my little nephew."

I listened in awe as he spoke. From the stories Jordan would tell me about his time as a cop, it seemed that gruesome stories like that were far more common than one might think.

The teen remained silent as he stood in front of the door with his back towards us, listening to Jules tell his story. I had a feeling he wasn't actually trying to get the door to open, but he stood still with his hand placed against the door handle.

"Have there been any more incidents like that?" the boy asked.

Jules shook his head. "I'm not sure. I quit the force not long after. I remember something similar happening not too long ago, though. A young girl, if I'm not mistaken."

There was a long pause, and I watched in silence as Bernie rubbed Jules' back in small circles with her hand.

"And there was nothing you could do about it because you didn't work there anymore," the boy said.

"No," Jules agreed. "I was long gone by then."

Another long pause. My sight wasn't too great

through the crack, but I could faintly see the kid's hand clenching and unclenching against the door.

"And you didn't stop him from leaving? You didn't insist he stay so he could help more people?" he said to the woman.

Bernie started a moment, then paused. "Well, no. I encouraged him to leave, actually. It did horrendous things to his well-being."

The room filled with silence after she spoke, and I could hear my heart beat again through my chest.

The boy suddenly turned back towards the room with a big smile spread across his face. "How do you like the drinks? It's my mother's recipe. One of our family's favorites. Do you like it?"

Bernie and Jules sipped their glasses politely and nodded.

"Oh, yes," Bernie said. "It's lovely. What a curious flavor. What is in it?"

The boy's smile turned into a sideways grin. "Secret family recipe. Drink up, I've got lots left and no one to share it with. The limo should be here any minute." He glanced out of the window quickly, and then smiled back at the couple as they took another sip. "Any minute, indeed."

The woman raised her hand to her forehead and leaned in toward her partner. "I'm feeling a bit woozy. Maybe I shouldn't drink too much before we eat."

A moment later Jules sidestepped as he nearly lost his balance. "Me, too. What's in this drink?"

"Secret family recipe," the boy repeated, smiling at the pair as they swayed on their feet, clutching to each other's bodies for support. "Don't worry, it will all be over soon."

The sound of a glass shattering echoed through the room as Bernie collapsed onto the floor.

A moment later, Jules collapsed next to her, and both bodies were lying still on the floor.

"Go, go, go!" Sheriff Reese shouted, and raised his gun as he ran around the back wall and into the adjoining room.

CHAPTER SIXTEEN

"Put your hands where I can see them!" the sheriff shouted as we ran into the room.

I bolted after him, running towards the spot where the couple had collapsed on the ground, but Jordan held out his arm and held me back. "Stay back, we don't know what he's capable of."

I looked down at the two forms on the ground and knew we didn't have much time. They didn't seem to be breathing, and I didn't know if they were even dead or alive.

The boy looked confused and simply stared at each of us in turn with a look of mild awe on his face.

Looking at him from this close, now, he looked like he could easily have been fifteen. What could have possibly happened to someone so young to hold this much hate in their heart?

"Hands in the air," Sheriff Reese shouted. He aimed his gun at the boy, and Brett did the same beside him.

The boy cocked an eyebrow and looked amused, then slowly began lowering the tray to the ground.

"Slowly," the sheriff said, watching his every movement with keen intent.

The boy placed the tray on the ground, and on his way back up he flicked the decanter over and spilled the contents on the floor.

"Oops," he said with a cheeky grin.

The clear liquid spread across the uneven floorboards towards the sheriff, and I noticed a strange shimmer to the surface of the spilled drink.

"Hands up where…" the sheriff teetered suddenly in place, and a strained expression spread across his face.

I looked around, and Brett, Jordan, and the other officers had the same woozy expression.

"Sheriff," I said. "What's going on? Are you alright?"

A moment later the sheriff collapsed to the ground, his face pressed up against the wet ground. His eyes remained open and were glazed over.

One by one the other men fell.

Brett was next, as he was next closest to the spilled liquid.

The other two officers followed, each landing with a loud thud on the ground.

Jordan fell next, and I did my best to catch him, but he fell like a dead weight and landed hard on the ground on his shoulder.

"The drink," Bailey said in a panic. "It's spelled."

"What did you do to them?" I shouted at the boy.

He grinned at me, the amused look growing even brighter on his face.

"My, my, what an interesting turn of events," he spat.

I was shaking Jordan by the shoulder, and Bailey had run over to Brett.

I shook and hit him, but he wouldn't move. I pressed the side of my face up to his to try and hear his breathing, but it was so faint I could hardly tell. I felt for his pulse, and it was there, albeit extremely faint.

"Why are you doing this?" I shouted at the boy. "What the hell is going on?"

The boy crossed his arms and raised his eyebrow at me. "Curious. Why didn't you both fall, too?"

I glared at him and continued to shake Jordan by the shoulder.

"Help!" I shouted at the top of my lungs, but it was no use. No one would hear us out there.

"Good luck calling for help here, lady," the boy said. "No one is going to hear you."

The spirits around me were in a mad panic, moving back and forth around the room, chattering excitedly amongst themselves. They no longer seemed scared, they were outright angry.

"Devil," I heard one shout. "Monster," another said. "You sick, twisted mother..." I didn't want to repeat the entire curse, but I could tell you it definitely wasn't polite.

"Ah," the boy finally said, realization dawning on his face. "You must be witches. Welcome, sisters."

I pushed myself up on my feet and balled my hands into fists. "We're no family of yours, you sick little monster."

"That's not very nice talk for someone who's trapped inside a room full of dead people. You don't want to join them, do you?"

My heart raced in my chest, and I motioned for Bailey to go look at the couple who had fallen before we arrived.

She crawled over to them, tears streaming down her face, and listened for their heart beats. She nodded up at me with a faint smile on her face. "They're still alive. Barely."

I sighed a loud sigh of relief. At least we had a small chance of getting everyone out alive. We just had to figure out what to do with the evil kid in front of us.

"They won't be alive for long," the boy said. "Their hearts grow weaker by the minute.

"Why are you doing this?" I demanded.

The boy laughed. "So curious, you are. No matter. I've got just the thing for you, two."

The kid spoke strangely for someone in his teens. He definitely didn't sound like he was local.

"Don't even think about moving," I snapped as the boy stepped towards his bag. "I've got a gun, and I'm not afraid to get it out."

The kid grinned. "I don't see a gun. I call a bluff."

I glanced down to the sheriff's still form. His gun was lying not too far away from him. If only I could just get close enough to grab it.

"Nuh-huh," the boy waggled his finger at me as I slowly sidestepped towards the sheriff.

I froze in place, glaring at him.

"Don't even think about it, lady. Look what I've done to all these people." He motioned around the room towards the dozens of spirits around us. "Don't you think I'm capable of doing the same to two more? Please."

I stepped back and reached my hand out towards Bailey who took it quickly and squeezed. At least we had each other.

"Funny," the boy said. "I don't remember inviting all of you. Who did you say you were?"

I continued to glare the boy, but neither of us spoke.

The boy sighed. "Pity. It will be a shame to have to get rid of both of you." He glanced down at the sheriff and the other officers, and his confidence wavered somewhat. "And it certainly isn't ideal to have gotten active duty cops. What a shame."

The boy turned his attention back to Bailey and me. "I suspect one of you is River Halloway, correct?"

We held our silence, and I squeezed Bailey's hand even harder. We both remained transfixed on the boy, and I was trying my best to come up with some sort of spell to use in case he decided to attack us.

He glanced down at the men around him on the floor. "And which one here is Jordan O'Riley?"

"None of your damn business," I snapped.

The boy raised his eyebrow again. He looked eerily like the Joker from batman, I noticed. All pale-skinned and wild-eyed. His mouth even did that weird lopsided grin. Looking at him sent shivers down my spine.

"Interesting. You must be River, then."

The boy raised his hands and began chanting an incantation.

I screamed and lunged toward him, tackling him down to the ground with a loud thud. I did my best to pin him down, but he proved to be stronger than I was, being a full head taller than I, and he wrestled me onto my back with barely any struggle at all.

"Why are you doing this?" I shouted at him,

wrestling against his strength. "What do you have against cops?"

The boy pushed me down onto my back again and pinned my shoulders down with the entire weight of his body. "Not cops," he snarled. "Retired cops. Cops who gave up on their communities. Pathetic weak people who abandoned those who need them most."

"What happened to you to hate them so much?" I said through gritted teeth. I pushed up against him, but couldn't make him move.

The boy screamed loudly and slapped me hard across the face.

"Shut up!" he yelled. "They deserve to be punished."

I grunted and called on all my strength, but it was no use, the boy had me pinned. I began screaming and thrashing, but still he held me down.

He grinned down at me with that eerie grin and continued his incantation, nearly spitting the words onto my face.

I didn't recognize what he was saying. It sounded like Latin to me, but whatever it was, I doubted it was going to end well.

"Bailey," I shouted. "Do something!"

I could see Bailey from the corner of my eye trying to tear up a floorboard to use as a weapon, but it was no use. A moment later, though, she reached into her bag and brought out Mrs. Brody's heavy little box.

She then threw the box as hard as she could, and it made contact with the back of the kid's head.

His eyes grew wide upon impact, and he slumped down on me heavily, completely unconscious.

CHAPTER SEVENTEEN

"Nice one," I said to her as I tried to wiggle free from under the boy's weight.

The box itself fell to the ground and shattered, spilling its magical contents into the room.

I regained my breath and pushed the boy the rest of the way off of me. Bailey came to help and rolled the boy into his side.

"The gun would have been a better choice, no?" I asked, pulling Bailey into a sideways hug.

Bailey shook her head. "I'm sorry. I panicked."

I shrugged. "Whatever, it worked. Thank you."

I rubbed my shoulder where I had hit the ground. It was extremely tender, and I had a feeling I would have a massive bruise.

"Quick," I said. "Pull the others away from the liquid. They might recover if we can get them fresh air."

Bailey and I dragged the unconscious bodies towards the outer walls of the mill, as far away from the spilled liquid as possible.

The ghosts watched us as we worked, but said nothing.

Finally, I approached one of the ghosts and asked if they had any advice. The male figure shook his head. "No, it's too late. They're gone."

I shook my head, refusing to believe it. "You're wrong. We can save them." Tears began streaming down my cheeks as I desperately tried to think of a way out of the situation we were in.

I brought out my phone all the while keeping an eye on the unconscious kid on the floor. He could wake up any minute, and we had to be ready.

I tried dialing 911, but there was no reception where we were.

I swore under my breath and ran to the other side of the building. Still, no signal.

"No wonder the sheriff wasn't answering our calls," I said to Bailey. "There's no damn reception here."

I gasped as the boy stirred, but after a moment he fell still again.

"We don't have much time," Bailey said in a panic. "What do we do?"

I looked around the room hoping that something would jump out at me with an idea.

I had grabbed the sheriff's gun and slid it into

my back pocket and Bailey did the same with Brett's, so at least we could protect ourselves if the boy awoke.

The guns wouldn't protect us from magic, though.

"The handcuffs," I said. "Grab the sheriff's handcuffs, and we'll cuff the kid in case he wakes up."

Bailey nodded. "Good idea."

Bailey grabbed the handcuffs from the sheriff's belt, and we snapped them around the boy's wrists. I then kicked the kid over onto his stomach so we wouldn't have to look at his evil face.

Bailey raised her eyebrow at me after I did so, and I shrugged. "To keep him from choking on his tongue," I said.

I felt strangely calm, and I noticed Bailey even had a large smile on her face.

I glanced around the room and realized what was happening.

"Oh crap," I said. "Bailey, Mrs. Brody's box. It's filling the entire space with its magic."

I began to hear the faint sound of sleigh bells and the smell of Christmas baking consumed me.

Bailey laughed. "Oh no. What do we do?"

The box was smashed into pieces on the floor, and we had no hope in containing the magic.

I jumped as the boy stirred again on the floor. This time he groaned and tried to move his arm.

Bailey and I stepped back from the kid. Sure, he was cuffed, but we still didn't know what sort of magic he was capable of.

As the kid groaned into the floor, I ran toward his bag and dragged it as far away from him as possible. Perhaps there would be something in the bag that would be useful.

"I'm going to look through here," I said. "You go try and call for help."

I began to giggle. Dammit, I couldn't help myself. The stupid holiday spirit in the room was too powerful. I could barely resist the urge to start singing. What the hell was happening to me? It was certainly the most inappropriate thing that could possibly have happened at that moment.

Bailey began humming a Christmas tune as she hopped between the unconscious bodies on the floor, checking to see if they were still alive.

"No one's dead yet," Bailey sang. "Their hearts are still beating. Barely, though."

She looked so unbelievably happy from the magic in the room as she pressed her cheek against Brett's chest. I couldn't believe the situation we had gotten ourselves into.

"What the hell is happening?" I shouted to the room around us. The ghosts nearby jumped away from me, but the holiday spirit in the room was too much for anyone to resist.

We were locked in an old mill with no hope of

getting out and calling for help. Our friends were lying on the ground dying, a murderous teenager was groaning on the floor in handcuffs, and we were dancing around humming Christmas tunes, the happiest we had been in a long time. Unintentionally happy, mind you. But happy none the less. What on earth was Mrs. Brody thinking, putting the box in Bailey's bag? That was certainly not the time for carol singing.

The sound of carols in my head began to grow louder, and I realized the spirits in the room had began to sing. Dammit.

Of course, it would affect them, too. It affected Sarah and Peter when Mrs. Brody opened the box on Christmas Eve, so it made sense it would have the same effect, here. Only, the effect was about tenfold, as the entire magical contents of the box filled the room.

At least it improved the mood in the room. The ghosts were no longer scared and angry, they were actually smiling and singing with each other.

I shook my head, trying to imagine what this scene would look like to an outsider. What a mess we had gotten ourselves into.

"Bailey," I finally said. "What are we going to do? We need to call for help, and fast! They're going to die without help."

Bailey laughed. "I know, it's awful. We need a plan." She smiled and began singing the Christmas

Song with the spirits around her. If she was concerned, she definitely didn't show it. I doubted I did, either, and felt immensely guilty for it.

I focused my attention back to the kid's bag I had in my hand and began looking through its contents to see if there was anything valuable we could use to get ourselves out of this mess. There must at least be a key or something for the door.

The bag contained mostly newspaper cut-outs and a notepad, and I dumped the entire contents of it onto the floor for a better look.

I recognized many of the people from the missing persons articles we had read, and many of their faces were cut out in the newspaper clippings. I looked up around me and recognized the spirits who matched the identities of the victims in the articles.

There wasn't much else in the bag apart from more clippings, a notebook, and a framed photo of a middle-aged couple. The male had the same lopsided grin as the kid, and I suspected they were his parents.

I looked through the papers on the ground and found a newspaper clipping with the matching photo, dated back to three years prior.

The couple had been murdered in their home during a break-in while their son hid in a closet. The kid had apparently called 911 a few times, but the local police officer - of which there was only one, apparently, in his tiny town - had recently retired and moved away with his girlfriend and they hadn't yet replaced him. By the time the state police arrived, the parents had been killed, and the suspect had escaped.

Well, crap. No wonder the kid had it out for retired cops.

I spread out the papers, hoping to find a key of some sort, but there was nothing like that that I could see.

I picked up the notebook and flipped through it, pausing on the first page that contained a list of scribbled names.

About halfway down the page, I read the names Jordan O'Riley with the word retired next to it and my name beside it.

I shook my head and wondered how the kid even knew we were together. He must have spent ages researching these people and their lives. As far as I knew, Jordan and my relationship wasn't really that public and his methods of finding out about us were really quite worrisome.

Not as worrisome as the dying bodies around me, though. I snapped the notebook shut and bent down next to Jordan. His face was growing more pale by the minute, and I began to panic as the realization that they might not actually make it came crashing down on me.

I stroked his hair and shook him again,

whispering his name into his ear. He lay still, completely unconscious and nonreactive.

"Help!" I finally shouted at the top of my voice. "Anyone, please! Help!"

Bailey shouted as well, and we both yelled at the top of our lungs. It was no use, though, as no one could hear us in such a remote location.

About an hour passed since the box broke and the magic was released, and the power of the spell was just getting stronger. Mistletoe was sprouting along the walls and roof beams, and I swore the air was sparkling.

I tried my best to ignore my surroundings, trying to focus on the people on the floor and a way out, but the environment was distracting and all I could think about was eggnog and Santa Clause.

"UGH!" I shouted angrily. Well, it came out sounding cheerful, but deep down I was angry.

I ran towards the door and began kicking it and shaking it, hoping that maybe the latches would break or something.

I whispered a small incantation to break the lock, but the spell zapped back at me and shocked my face with its strange reaction. The kid must have spelled the door. Of course, he would, given the lengths he seemed to have gone to lure those poor people to the mill.

I glanced up towards the ceiling as snow began to

fall inside the room. Mrs. Brody's magic was strong, and the entire mill began to look some crazy scene from a Christmas movie. I shook my head and brushed the snow off my shoulders, trying my best to ignore the sounds and smells emanating from all around me.

I finally had to cover my ears with my hands and fell to my knees, shouting for help repeatedly until I felt like I was going to pass out.

I jumped back a moment later as I noticed one of the thin windows illuminate with light from outside. I tried to listen through the sounds of Christmas, but I couldn't really hear anything past the growing sound of sleigh bells and music.

The light got brighter, then instantly turned off.

I ran towards Bailey, panicked. "It's a car. Someone is outside!"

Bailey's eyes grew wide with fear. "Do you think it's another couple?" she asked.

I shrugged. "I don't know. It could be an accomplice of his. We have no way of knowing."

"Quick, behind the wall!" We nearly had to shout through the loud sounds in the room. Whoever was outside was going to be met with an exceptionally strange scene when they came in.

We both held our breaths as we watched the front door through the cracks in the wall.

The doors slowly opened, and three silhouettes appeared in the doorway. As they stepped closer into the room, I breathed a sigh of relief as I recognized the blue of Mrs. Brody's hair.

Bailey and I ran back around the other side of the wall to greet them.

"Don't close the door!" I shouted.

The door nearly closed, but Jane reached back and grabbed it before it shut.

"It locks from the inside. We were locked in!" I managed to say through heavy breathing once I ran all the way across the mill to join them.

"What are you doing here?" Bailey exclaimed.

I couldn't believe our luck. Maybe we weren't going to die in this Christmassy prison, after all.

Jane removed her shoe and used it to prop the door open. "When you guys didn't answer your phones, we suspected something was wrong."

"Any then Mrs. Brody sensed her spell was released, and we really knew something was going down," Rory said.

"But how did you get here?" I asked. "How did you know where we were?"

Mrs. Brody rolled her eyes. "You girls constantly underestimate me."

"Do you track us?" I asked, shocked.

Mrs. Brody shrugged and gazed about the room.

I walked up to one of the windows and stood on my tiptoes to look out of it. I cupped my hands around my eyes to block out the light and looked out to see Brett's car outside.

"How did you use Brett's car without the key?" I asked.

"What did I just say, dear?" Mrs. Brody exclaimed. "I have my ways. Don't you worry about it."

Rory stepped into the room with a blended look of both terror and awe.

"What the hell happened here?" she asked. She then pointed at the shifting half-conscious teenage boy on the floor. "And who is he?"

I walked up to the boy and bent down to see his face. His eyes were closed, but he shifted and groaned, and I suspected he was slowly coming to.

"The one responsible for all of this," I spat.

Rory stepped away from him, the look on her face turning to one of complete disgust.

Mrs. Brody, quite the sight to see in her favorite brown nightgown and electric blue spiky hair, stepped into the center of the room and took in the scene around her. She then looked to the side wall and noticed the still forms of the Jordan, Brett, the sheriff, his two officers, and the couple, and frowned. "Well, let's do something about this, shall we?"

CHAPTER EIGHTEEN

Good old Mrs. Brody always knew what to do in the strangest of situations. She waved her hands, and at least the snow stopped falling inside, but the rest of the spell was still running full-force.

The spirits were singing, and the air still smelled like cookies, but at least we could see now without the thick falling snow.

I led Mrs. Brody towards the couple, and she kneeled down next to them and began inspecting their bodies.

"They drank straight from the potion that did this," I explained. "They were the first ones down. Everyone else just inhaled it after he dumped it on the floor."

Mrs. Brody nodded. "Alright. Thank you, dear. Will you be so kind as to go get my bag from the car?"

"I'll get it," Bailey said, and she sprinted out through the doors towards the car. She came back a moment later with a tiny purse, no bigger than a satchel.

"Just set it down over there, dear," Mrs. Brody said, pointing near the spilled liquid on the ground. Most of it had dripped through the cracks between the floorboards, but there was still enough for her to go investigate its contents.

She walked over to the puddle and dipped her finger in the liquid. She then sniffed it and gave it a quick lick.

I recoiled at the sight and really hoped she knew what she was doing. The last thing we needed was an unconscious Mrs. Brody to top off the events of the evening.

Fortunately, she didn't seem affected by the magic, and she tasted the liquid a few more times before figuring out what the contents were.

"Clever," she murmured as she worked.

"What is it?" I asked. I wished she would hurry up. Jordan's face was growing paler by the minute, and I wasn't sure how much time he had left.

I could appreciate the benefit of the stupid Christmas spell, as under any other circumstance I would be absolutely catatonic at that moment, watching my boyfriend slowly fade away. As chance had it, while I was obviously concerned, the spell was so all-consuming that my heart wasn't breaking nearly as much as it should have been.

If he did die and the spell wore off... Well, that would be another thing, entirely.

"It's a combination of a sleeping draught, a paralytic, and a touch of foxglove to stop the heart."

"Witches clove?" I asked, shocked. My father had taught me all about different herbs and their uses when I was young. Foxglove, or witch's clove, was one that he taught me to avoid at all cost, as it was extremely poisonous and could kill you if consumed. I remember that one in particular, because the flowers were so pretty, and I would often bring them home for my aunt in a bouquet. That was until I learned how deadly it was.

Maybe that was why they stopped inviting me home for the holidays.

Mrs. Brody nodded and began looking through her tiny satchel. She then pulled out a few glass containers and set them on the ground around her and began filling them with various liquids and crushed herbs from her bag.

I watched her in wonder, curious how so many large items could fit in such a small bag. Magic was absolutely amazing, sometimes. Even growing up in a house full of magic and spells, some things still blew me away. I watched her pull item after item out of that tiny bag, and couldn't help but think of Harry Potter.

"Cool," I whispered.

After a few minutes of furious mixing and measuring, Mrs. Brody held out a vial of clear purple liquid.

"This should do the trick," she said. She handed me the vial, and I ran over towards Jordan. I then stopped and turned and ran towards the couple instead, knowing full well that they needed it more than he did. It was a hard decision, but the right one.

"Just a drop will do, dear," Mrs. Brody said.

I tilted the woman's chin up and spilled a small amount of the liquid into her throat. Within seconds she was coughing frantically and rolled onto her side panting. I beamed up at Mrs. Brody who nodded and went to join the spirits watching us from the other side of the room.

I gave some of the antidote to the man, and he joined his partner in a fit of coughs. They were alive, which was the good part, but they didn't look to be too healthy. And they would likely need some serious counseling, I imagined.

"Can any of you go call for help, now? There's no reception here," I asked. "I have a feeling the sheriff might need a hand when this is all said and done."

Rory nodded. "I'll drive down the road until we can get reception. Be back shortly."

"I'll come with," Jane said.

The two girls left the mill, and I heard the car

drive away. With any luck, the local police would arrive and deal with the mess on their own.

When I was sure the couple would be alright, I ran towards Jordan and dumped some of the liquid down his throat.

He sputtered and coughed immediately, and looked up me and smiled when he finally caught his breath.

"Welcome back," I said to him. He tried to say something, but couldn't quite make out the words through his coughing.

I kissed his cheek and went to Brett next. Bailey was sitting next to him and held his hand as he regained consciousness. He looked confused at the fact that she had his hands in his, but he just smiled up at her and let her hold him.

I then revived the sheriff and his officers, and after a few minutes, everyone was up and breathing normally.

"Is everyone okay?" I asked.

Nearly everyone looked confused and distraught, but at least they were alive. I gave Jordan a hug and helped pull him to his feet.

Sheriff Reese pushed himself up as well and ran over to the kid on the floor.

The teenager had rolled onto his back and was glaring up at the ceiling.

"You've got a lot of explaining to do, kid," the

sheriff said angrily to him. "You're not going to see the light of day some time."

It didn't take long for Jane and Rory to come back, followed by the flashing lights of two cop cars.

Three state police officers stormed in but stopped abruptly when they noticed the strange Christmassy scene in front of them.

"What's going on here?" one particularly rough-looking officer demanded.

I walked up to them and began explaining the situation, everything from Jordan's invitation, to the teenager who met the couple at the mill. I left out the bits about the ghosts and the magic, in case they weren't familiar with that sort of thing. I needed them to believe us to be sane, and flaunting strange magic to non-magic people often ended poorly.

Fortunately, one of the officers stepped forward and looked up at the spreading mistletoe on a beam above him.

He grinned. "Magic?"

I nodded slowly, waiting for him to add more.

"It's okay," he said. "My brother's wife is a witch. We're familiar with that sort of thing. Deal with it a lot at work."

I smiled. "Oh good, then I've got more to tell you."

The three officers listened intently to my story, and Sheriff Reese chimed in when necessary. He seemed more than happy to pass off this case to someone else, and once we had finished explaining everything to the officers, they re-cuffed the kid with their own handcuffs and took him away.

We watched as the teenager was dragged from the mill, and I let out a deep breath I hadn't notice I was holding.

"Kid's a witch," Sheriff Reese said to the officer with the witch sister-in-law. "Better get in some extra help in that regard, if you need it."

The officer hung back and shook the sheriff's hand. "Thanks for your hard work, sheriff. We'll take it from here."

"Oh wait," I said. "You'll want these. They belong to him." I collected the newspaper clippings and things from the ground and placed them back in the bag and handed it to the officer. He smiled and nodded and turned to the couple who were standing quietly apart from the group.

"You two should come with me," he said softly. "We'll get you looked at. I'm sure we'll have some questions for you, as well."

Bernie and Jules nodded and followed the officer out the door.

We all stood in silence a moment, unsure what to do next. I glanced around the room at the spirits and the explosion of holiday spirit everywhere. Days like this didn't happen to just anyone.

"Well, that's that," Jordan said as the outer doors

shut. Rory held the inner door open so we wouldn't get locked in again.

I shook my head. "What do we do about all the ghosts?" The spirits had gathered near the center of the room, watching us curiously. They no longer seemed scared, and a few had even struck up a conversation with Mrs. Brody.

When we had all collected our things and gotten ready to leave, two young-looking spirits approached me.

"Did Sarah and Peter find you?" the woman asked. "I used to work with Peter, and Sarah and I were friends from way back."

I smiled at her and nodded. "Yes, they did. They're the reason we came."

The male spirit smiled back at me. "That's fortunate. You guys saved those two people, today. Thank you."

"I only wish we could have done more," I answered. "What are you going to do now?"

The couple looked at each other and then back at me. "Can we come with you to see Sarah and Peter?"

I thought for a moment and shrugged. "I don't see why not. I'm not sure how you'll get there. I'm afraid I don't know too much about spirit travel."

The girl shrugged. "It's okay, we'll figure it out."

I told them our address and explained how to find the house, and they seemed content with that and left to rejoin the other spirits in the middle of the room.

I turned to Mrs. Brody who had wandered over to where I stood. "Can you reverse the spell he cast on this place?"

"Of course, I can, dear," she answered. Mrs. Brody then scrunched up her face and muttered an incantation, and the walls of the mill wavered for a moment. I could feel a tension I hadn't even noticed in the room disappear.

"You can all leave now," Mrs. Brody called to the room. "Go find your peace, dears."

The spirits were reluctant, but after the first couple passed through the door without any problem, the rest followed suit.

I had no idea where they were all going to do, but I imagined it would be a relief to finally be let out of the place where you had been killed. What a horrible thing to have happen, and to have to stay in the location of your murder after you die and witness more innocent people meet the same fate? I couldn't imagine anything worse.

"Shall we go home?" I asked Mrs. Brody.

She nodded. "Yes, dear. Let's go home.

WE ALL PILED into the cars we had come in, with the exception of Brett who insisted on driving his own car back. He seemed none too impressed that they had hijacked his car, although given the events of the evening he didn't actually seem too angry about it. Bailey rode shotgun with Brett, and Mrs. Brody and Jane went with Rory.

Sheriff Reese and his officers took their car and the sheriff insisted I meet with him in the next few days to go over what had happened. For just then, though, he was content going home to some peace and quiet for a while.

I couldn't think of anything I wanted more.

I drove home with Jordan, and I held his hand most of the way. I couldn't bring myself to tell him how scared I was that he might have died. Oh, sure, the stupid holiday spirit helped keep my spirits up - pun intended - but deep down I knew how devastated I would have been if I had lost him.

He seemed to read my emotions without me having to say anything, though, and he just kept squeezing my hand as he drove us home.

We arrived back at the house about an hour later, and we all gathered around the fire in the living room to unwind from the craziness of the day.

Sarah and Peter were hanging around by the tree when we arrived, watching the cats play in front of the warmth from the fire. Momma's new little kitten was beyond adorable, and it chased Agnes around in circles as we all watched.

"We found friends of yours," I finally said to Sarah and Peter as everyone settled.

Sarah looked excitedly at me, but then her expression turned dark. "Oh. As ghosts, you mean?"

"Yes. I'm sorry," I said. "But they said they would come by and see you."

Sarah smiled. "Oh, that's nice. Something to look forward to."

Bailey, Rory, and Jane began singing Christmas carols again, and I snuggled into the couch next to Jordan, content just to listen in silence for a while. Brett sat on the other end of the couch, and Soot jumped up on his lap and curled up. He smiled and pet the cat, and I realized I would have revisit my opinion of him. Bailey kept looking over at him with big puppy-dog eyes, and I had a feeling we would be seeing quite a lot of Brett in the following weeks.

I supposed he wasn't such a bad guy, after all. Everyone had bad days, right?

After about the third song the girls sang, curiosity got the better of me. "Mrs. Brody. What's going to happen to the holiday spirit?"

She smirked but said nothing.

"No, really," I insisted. "Will it just disappear?"

Mrs. Brody shook her head. "You can't get rid of holiday spirit, dear. Spirit is contagious if you haven't noticed." She motioned around the room, and I saw how happy and joyful everyone looked.

"I suppose," I said. "But what does that mean for the mill?"

Mrs. Brody considered a moment. "I imagine it will just keep getting stronger and growing."

My mouth fell open. "Forever?"

Mrs. Brody shrugged. "Well, I should expect so, yes."

I laughed and tried to imagine someone visiting the mill in the middle of summer, only to be met by Christmas carols, mistletoe, and the smell of fresh-baked Christmas cookies.

What a strange and wonderful world we lived in.

"I'm sorry you lost your spell," I finally said.

"Oh, don't be ridiculous, dear. It's not gone. Look around us."

I looked around the room and didn't see anything at first. But after a moment I could faintly hear the sleigh bells and could feel my heart warm with the same strange feeling I had felt earlier.

"See? You can't escape holiday spirit. It can only just grow and grow."

A smirk spread across my face at the sheer ridiculousness of the situation. That woman had a knack for making the ordinary extraordinary.

We all relaxed for an hour or two, and eventually, everyone bid each other goodnight. Brett said his goodbyes, exchanged phone numbers with Bailey, and left to drive back to Boston. Mrs. Brody insisted he stay, but he was eager to leave. The events of the day would have been a lot to handle for him, I imagined.

Jordan decided to go home, too, so he could get some sleep and then go visit his parents first thing in the morning.

I walked him outside to say goodbye, away from prying eyes.

He took my hand and led be to the back of the house, where we had first really connected a few months before.

Snow had begun to fall again, and the Christmas lights on the lighthouse way out in the bay were reflecting across the water in beautiful shimmery bands of red and green.

I noticed the smell of baking cookies and laughed as I realized there was no escaping Mrs. Brody's Christmas spirit.

"Do you know how to do any holiday normally?" Jordan asked me.

I shook my head. "Apparently not since moving here. I think next year I'll just go to Mexico."

Jordan laughed. "Sounds like a plan."

He squeezed my hands in his and I gazed into his ice blue eyes and finally felt a moment of the perfect peace and quiet I had hoped for over the holidays.

We both looked up as we noticed a bough of mistletoe spreading on the roof above us.

I looked back into Jordan's eyes, and he kissed me.

"Merry Christmas, River," he murmured against my lips.

What a strange and awful yet glorious holiday this had been.

I couldn't help the smile that threatened to take over my face. "Merry Christmas."